KALIFRIKI

Hard Cover ISBN 13: 978-1-5154-5400-7
E-book ISBN 13: 978-1-5154-5401-4

KALIFRIKI

ROGER ZELAZNY

OTHER WORKS BY ROGER ZELAZNY

Lord of Light
Roadmarks
The Last Defender of Camelot
The Dead Man's Brother
Creatures of Light and Darkness
The Magic
Shadows & Reflections
Doorways in the Sand
Manna from Heaven
My Name is Legion
A Night in the Lonesome October
Dilvish the Damned
The Changing Land
Today we Choose Faces
Bridge of Ashes
Home is the Hangman
Night Kings and Night Heirs

Chronicle of Amber
Nine Princes in Amber
The Guns of Avalon
The Hand of Oberon
Sign of the Unicorn
The Courts of Chaos
Blood of Amber
Trumps of Doom
Sign of Chaos
Knight of Shadows
Prince of Chaos
Seven Tales in Amber

KALIFRIKI OF THE THREAD

Tops of different sorts, and jointed dolls,
and fair, golden apples frotn the clear-voiced Hesperides . . . .
—ORPHEUS THE THRACIAN

This is the story of Kalifriki of the Thread, the Kife, and the toymaker's daughter—in the days of the shifter's flight from the Assassin's Garden, wherefrom it bore a treasure almost without price. But even a Kife can be followed by a Master of the Thread. For the Thread may wander anywhere and need not have an end; the Thread has more sides than a sword; the Thread is subtle in its turnings, perhaps infinite in the variations it may play in the labyrinths of doom, destiny, desire. No one, however, can regard every turning of fate from the Valley of Frozen Time. Attempts to do so tend to terminate in madness.

When the man tracked the Kife to the ice-feik and slew it there, the Kife knew it was in trouble, for it was the third time the man had reached it, the third world upon which he had found it, and the third time that he had slain it, a feat none had ever accomplished before.

Now, five times in a year is the charm for destruction of a Kife, and it seemed that this one suspected as much, for he had managed the pursuit as none had ever done before. The Kife did not understand how the man had located it and reached it, and it realized it was important that it learn as much as possible before the lights went out.

So it stared at the hunter—hammer jawed, high of cheek, dark eyed beneath an oddly sensitive brow, dark hair tied back with a strip of blue cloth. The man still held the trident which had emitted the vibrations that had shattered several of the Kife's major organs, one of the few portable weapons capable of dispatching it from the high dragon form with such ease. The man wore mittens, boots, and a heavy white garment of fur, the hood thrown back now.

6

The midnight sun stood behind his head, and stars glittered like ice moths beside his shoulders.

"And again it is you," the Kife hissed.

The other nodded. The Kife noted a slight irregularity to the man's lower teeth, a small scar beside his right eye, a piece of red thread wrapped about his left wrist.

"What is your name?" the Kife asked him.

"I am called Kalifriki," said the man.

"How do you do what you do?"

For the first time, the man smiled.

"I might ask the same of you," he replied.

"Shifter's secret," the Kife answered.

"To all tricks their trades," said the man.

"And why you?" the Kife asked.

Kalifriki continued to smile. If he replied, the Kife did not hear it. It felt the death seize and squeeze, and as the world went away it saw the man reach to touch the Thread.

Kalifriki watched as the body collapsed, fuming, leaving him with only the green and silver-scaled hide. As the essence emerged, he reached forward and trailed the Thread through it. At that moment, it was difficult to see precisely where the strand began or ended. The man's gaze followed it into the smoky distance, and then he moved.

There is a timeless instant where the world hangs frozen before you. It is map, sculpture, painting; it is not music, words, or wind. You may survey the course of your Thread through its time and space, attempt a rapid adjustment. Then the ice of Time is broken, the flow tugs at the strand of your existence, and you are drawn into the game.

*

The Kife came to consciousness without breaking the rhythm of its six arms as they chipped delicately at the mineral encrustations. The sky was black above its burnished head, gem-quality stars strewn wherever it looked. Frost came and went upon its body surfaces, dialogue of thermostat and environment.

It had not had time to choose well because of the conversation preceding its departure from the other world. This shifting had almost been a shot in the dark. Almost.

But not quite. Here, there was a little mental trick, a tuning . . . .

Yes.

It could reach back into the larger brain, shielded within a distant cave, which oversaw the operation of the entire robot prospecting team. The brain operated at perhaps 10 percent of capacity. It drowsed. It almost sleepwalked its charges through their chores. But this was sufficient. The job was, in this fashion, adequately performed. If more brain work were needed, it would rise to the occasion. Only—

It infiltrated several circuits, then paused. There was no resistance. Like a rising tide, it flowed farther, ebbed, flowed, ebbed. The processor in the cave drowsed on. The Kife saw that it had long ago set alarms. So long as nothing interfered with the robot team's collection of minerals, it was content to contemplate a randomized hypothesis program it had designed, called "dreaming." Perceiving this, the Kife extended the rest of itself into the thinking space it required.

Now, now there were places beyond the routines, room to manipulate memories and ideas, to reason, to imagine at levels none of the other robots could achieve.

The Kife recalled the man who had slain it a world away. It remembered how the telepathic hunting pack, the Necrolotti, had fled from the man, having sensed a predator more dangerous than themselves. The man Kalifriki was a hunter, a killer, with the ability to traverse the side-by-side lands. It struck the Kife then that the two of them had much in common. But it did not believe that the man was of its own kind. That is, he shifted, but the means he employed bore no resemblance to the Kife's own methods.

It pondered the hunter's motives. Vengeance? For any of the numerous acts which might have gained it the hatred of someone it had underestimated? It thought then of their duel on the world before the ice-feik. No, there was no passion there. If someone wanted vengeance, it had to be some other, which, of course, would make the man a professional at the business.

Recovery? The man might be after it to obtain a thing it had taken. The Kife sought, in its hip compartment, after the item it had transformed considerable dragon-mass to energy in order to transport. Yes, it was intact. It occurred to it then that a mission of both vengeance and recovery was not out of the question. The one certainly did not preclude the other . . . .

But might it be made to? It toyed with the thought. It had died twice now because it had been surprised, and once because it had underestimated its adversary. And it had been surprised and had underestimated because so few creatures were truly a threat to Kife-kind. The Kife were rare in the side-by-side lands because of their ferocity. Each required a large range, and they kept their numbers low by means of quick, lethal, territorial disputes with each other. But beyond another Kife, there wasn't much that a Kife feared. Realistically, the Kife now added Kalifriki to the list. The man was particularly dangerous because the Kife was uncertain as to his motives or the full range of his abilities. Best to devote thought to ensuring against another surprise. But perhaps, just possibly, it should consider the terms of a bargain.

The days passed, barely distinguishable from the nights, and the Kife fell into the rock-harvesting routine. It conveyed the minerals to a truck, troubled only by the occasional seizing up of a limb. Twice, the truck's storage compartment was filled and the Kife drove it to the warehousing area where other robots unloaded it. The second time this was being done a servicing unit approached, fastened leads to sockets beneath its backplates, and performed a series of tests.

"You are due for a major overhaul," it broadcast. "We will send another to tend to your diggings and perform this servicing now."

"I am functioning fine, and I am in the midst of a complicated excavation," the Kife replied. "Do it next time."

"There is some leeway," the servicing unit admitted. "We will do it next time, as you say."

9

THE NIGHT KINGS AND NIGHT HEIRS

As the Kife headed back to its diggings it pondered a fresh dilemma. It could not permit itself to undergo a major servicing, for the special item it carried would be discovered and perhaps damaged during the course of it. Nor was the item the sort of thing it could merely hide for a long period of time.

The low temperatures which prevailed in this place would doubtless damage it.

Perhaps it were better simply to flee to another place. Only—

Only *this* might represent a problem. It had heard stories of shifters who could wait in the Valley of Frozen Time, watching another, waiting until that other moved to shift, and then pouncing. The Kife could not perform this feat, though it had often tried. The tale could well be apocryphal for it had also heard that that way lay madness. Stilt it were better not to underestimate the one called Kalifriki.

Therefore, it was better to remain at work. To remain, and to figure a means whereby it might manage the overhaul.

And so it slowed its pace, collecting minerals at half the rate it had earlier, saving wear and tear on its body and postponing another confrontation with a servicing unit. Stilt the call took it by surprise.

"Prospector unit, are you damaged?" came the broadcast message.

"I am not," it replied.

"You have been in the field much longer than usual. Is there a problem?"

"The work goes slowly."

"Perhaps the vein has been played out and you should be relocated."

"I think not. I have just uncovered a fresh deposit."

"It has been a long while since you have been overhauled."

"I know."

"Therefore, we are sending a mobile unit to your diggings, to service you in the field."

"That will not be necessary. I will be coming in before."

"You are beyond the safety limit. We will dispatch a mechanic unit."

KALIFRIKI OF THE THREAD

The transmission ended. The Kife made a decision. It was difficult to estimate when the service unit would arrive. But it was determined to undergo the servicing rather than flee. This required that it secrete the item. At least, it had discovered a means for preserving it outside its own body for a brief while, with the recent discovery of a cave subjected to geothermal heating by way of a deep pit in its floor.

It departed the work area, traveling to the opening in the side of a fractured ridge. Wisps of steam moved about it, and when the ground rumbled lightly these puffed more forcefully toward the heavens. It flicked on its dome light as it worked its way into the opening and entered the chamber where the pit glowed red-orange and gravel occasionally rattled across the floor. It halted at the rim, staring downward. The level of the bubbling magma seemed somewhat higher, but not so much so as to represent a danger to anything left in the chamber. Nor, according to its sensors, was there an increase in seismic activity since the time it had discovered this opening. Yes, this would be an ideal place to store it for a few hours while—

There came a flash of light from the entranceway, and its sensors read heat overload as one of its forelimbs was fused. Turning, it beheld a humanoid figure in a pressurized suit, light in one hand, pistol in the other. It also noted the strand of red wrapped around the figure's forearm.

"Kalifriki!" It broadcast on the wavelength used for general communication in this place. "Hold your fire or you may defeat your own purposes."

"Oh?" The man answered at the same frequency. "When did you become aware of my purposes?"

"You were not hired simply to destroy me, but to recover something I took, were you not?"

"Actually, I was hired to do both," Kalifriki replied.

"Then it was the Old Man of Alamut who retained you?"

"Indeed. When the Assassins need to hire an assassin they come to Kalifriki. "

"Would you consider making a deal?"

"Your life for the vial? No, I'd rather collect the entire fee."

"I was not really offering. I was merely curious," said the Kife, uwhether you would accept."

Kalifriki's weapon flared as the Kife charged him.

Two more of its six forearms were melted by the bright discharge, and a large block of sensors was destroyed. This meant very little to the Kife, however, for it felt it could spare considerable function and still remain superior to a human. In fact—

"It was foolish of you to follow me here," it said, as it swung a blow that missed Kalifriki but pulverized a section of the cave wall. "Another robot is even now on the way."

"No," the man replied. "I faked that call to get you to come here."

"You *chose* this place? Why?"

"I was hoping you'd have produced the vial by the time I arrived," he replied, diving to his right to avoid another charge. "Unfortunately, my entry was a trifle premature. Pity."

He fired again, taking out several more sensors and a square foot of insulation. The Kife turned with incredible speed, however, knocking the pistol upward and lunging. Kalifriki triggered the weapon in that position, threw himself to the rear and rolled, dropping his light as he did so. A section of the cave's roof collapsed, half burying the Kife, blocking the entranceway.

Kalifriki rose to his feet.

"I can take a terrific beating in this body," the Kife stated, beginning to dig itself out, "and still destroy you. Whereas the slightest damage to that suit means your end."

"True," said the man, raising the weapon and pointing it once again.

"Fortunately for me, that problem is already solved."

He pulled the trigger and the weapon crackled feebly and grew still.

"Oh," said the Kife, wishing his robot features capable of a smile.

Kalifriki holstered the weapon, raised a boulder, and hurled it. It smashed against the Kife's head and rolled off to the side where it fell into the pit. The

Kife increased its efforts to uncover itself, working with only two appendages, as the fourth of its arms had been damaged in the rockfall.

Kalifriki continued to hurl rubble as the Kife dug itself out. Charging the man then, the Kife reached for his throat. Its left arm slowed, emitted a grating noise, and grew still. The right arm continued toward Kalifriki, who seized it with both hands and ducked beneath it, springing to the robot's side, then again to its rear. The Kife's treads left the ground in the light gravity of the moonlet. As it was turned and tipped, it felt a push. Then it was falling, the glow rushing up toward it. Before it struck the magma it realized that it had underestimated Kalifriki again.

*

The Kife regarded the Valley of Frozen Time. As always, it tried to stretch the timeless moment wherein it could consider the physical prospects and some of the sequences available to it. For reasons it did not understand, the hovering process continued. It rejoiced, in that this time it saw the means whereby it might plot and manipulate events to an extent it had never achieved before. This time, not only would it be able to lay a trap for Kalifriki, but it would create one of subtlety and refinement, by a shifter, for a shifter, worthy of a shifter in all respects.

It was able to hold back the flow until almost everything was in place.

*

As Kalifriki followed the Thread through the placeless time into the timeless place, he was puzzled by its course thereafter, into the world to which he was about to follow the Kife for their final confrontation. It ran through the most unusual pattern he had ever beheld. It was too complicated a thing for him to analyze in detail before its force drew him to the level of events. Therefore, he would have to trust the instincts which had served him so well in the past, regarding the array only in gross, seeking the nexus of greatest menace and providing a lifeline of some sort. Here, he would have chuckled—though laughter, like wind or music, could not manifest in this place. He twisted the strand and whipped it, the hot, red loop following his will, racing away from him among canyons and boulevards of his latest world-to-be. He followed . . .

*

. . . Setting foot upon the rocky trail which gave way immediately beneath him. He reached for the passing ledge and caught hold, only to have it, too, yield as his weight came upon it. Then, through risen dust, he beheld the long, steep slope below, with several rocky prominences near which he soon must pass. He raised his left arm to protect his face, let his body go limp, and attempted to steer the course of descent with his heels as he reflected upon the prudence of dealing with a great and distant menace while neglecting a smaller but nasty one so close at hand.

*

When he woke he found himself in a large, canopied bed, his head aching, his mouth dry. The room was dark, but daylight leaked about the edges of shutters on the far wall. He attempted to rise so as to visit the window, but the pain in his right leg told him that a bone could be broken. He cursed in Norman French, Arabic, Italian, and Greek, wiped his brow, fell to musing, and passed back to sleep.

When next he woke it was to the singing of birds and the soft sounds of another's presence in the room. Through slitted eyelids, he beheld a human-sized form advancing upon him, areas of brightness moving at its back. It halted beside the bed, and he felt a cold hand upon his brow, fingertips at the pulse in his wrist. He opened his eyes.

She was blonde and dark eyed with a small chin, her face entirely unlined, expressionless in her attention. It was difficult for him to estimate whether she was tall, short, or somewhere between, in that he was uncertain as to the height of the bed. Behind her stood a gleaming simulacrum of an ape, an upright, bronze-plated chimpanzee, perfectly formed in every detail, bearing a large, dark case in its right hand. On the floor beside it stood a huge, silver tortoise, a covered tray on its back, its head turning slowly from side to side.

Only for an instant did the metallic bodies cause a rush of apprehension, as he recalled his battle with the Kife in its robot form.

14

Then, "Do not be distressed," he heard her say, in a language close to one of the many he spoke. "We wish only to help you."

"It was a memory come to trouble me," he explained. "Is my leg broken?"

"Yes," she replied, uncovering it. He beheld an ornate swirl of black-and-yellow metal about his lower right leg. It seemed a work of art, such as might be displayed at the Byzantine Court. "Dr. Shong set it," she added, indicating the metal ape, who bowed.

"How long ago was this?" Kalifriki asked.

She glanced at Dr. Shong, who said, "Three days—no, three and a half," in a voice like a brassy musical instrument played low and slow.

"Thank you. How did I come to this place?"

"We found you on one of our walks," Dr. Shong said, "mixed in with the remains of a rock slide, beneath a broken trail. We brought you back here and repaired you."

"What is this place?" he asked.

"This is the home of the toymaker, Jerobee Clockman, my father," the lady told him. "I am Yolara."

The question in her eyes and voice was clear.

"I am called Kalifriki," he said.

"Are you hungry, Kalifriki?" she asked.

He nodded, licking his lips. The smell of the food had become almost unbearable. "Indeed," he replied.

Dr. Shong raised him into a seated position and propped him with pillows while Yolara uncovered the tray and brought it to the bedside. She seated herself on an adjacent chair and offered him the food.

"Still warm," he observed, tasting it.

"Thank Odas," she said, gesturing toward the tortoise. "He bears a heating element in his back."

Odas met his gaze and nodded, acknowledging his thanks with, "My pleasure," rendered in a high, reedy voice, and, "Come Doctor," he continued, "let us leave them to organic converse unless we may be of some further service."

Yolara shook her head slightly and the pair departed.

When he finally paused between mouthfuls, Kalifriki nodded in the direction the pair had taken. "Your father's work?" he inquired.

"Yes," she answered.

"Ingenious, and lovely. Are there more such about?"

"Yes," she answered, staring at him so steadily as to make him uncomfortable. "You will meet more of them, by and by."

"And your father?"

"He is, at the moment, ill. Else he would have overseen your awakening and welcomed you in person."

"Nothing serious, I hope."

She looked away replying, "It is difficult to know. He is a reticent man."

"What of your mother?"

"I never knew her. Father says that she ran away with a Gypsy musician when I was quite young."

"Have you brothers or sisters?"

"None."

Kalifriki continued eating.

"What were you doing in these parts?" she asked after a time. "We are fairly remote from the avenues of commerce."

"Hunting," he said.

"What sort of beast?"

"It is rare. It comes from a place very far from here."

"What does it look like?"

"Anything."

"Dangerous?"

"Very."

"How is it called?"

"Kife."

She shook her head.

"I have never heard of such a creature."

"Just as well. When do you think I might get up?"

"Whenever you possess the strength. Dr. Shong says that the device you wear should protect your leg fully—though you might want a stick, for balance."

He lowered his fork

"Yes, I would like to try . . . soon," he said.

Shortly, she removed the tray and drew the cover higher, for he had fallen asleep.

When he woke that afternoon, however, he attempted to get up after eating. Dr. Shong rushed to assist him. While Yolara fetched a stick, the ape helped him to dress, performing neurological tests and checking his muscle tone during their frequent pauses. Dr. Shong picked away the Thread that clung to Kalifriki's wrist and tossed it aside. He did not see it drift back several moments later, settling upon his own shoulder, depending toward his hip.

They were halfway across the room when Yolara returned with the stick. Both accompanied him outside then and along the corridor to a balcony, whence he looked down upon a courtyard containing six sheep, two goats, four cows, a bull, and a flock of chickens, all fashioned of metals both dull and gleaming, all seeming to browse and forage, all producing peculiar approximations of the sounds made by their flesh-and-blood models.

"Amazing," Kalifriki stated.

"They are merely decorative machines, not possessed of true intellect," Dr. Shong observed. "They are but child's play for the Master."

"Amazing, nevertheless," said Kalifriki.

Yolara took his arm to steady him as he turned away, heading back inside.

"We'll return you to your room now," she said.

"No," he replied, turning toward a stairwell they had passed on their way up the hall. "I must go farther."

"Not stairs. Not yet," said Dr. Shong.

"Please do as he says," she asked. "Perhaps tomorrow."

"Only if we may walk to the far end of the hallway and back"

She glanced at the metal simian, who nodded.

"Very well. But let us go slowly. Why must you push yourself so hard?"

"I must be ready to face the Kife, anywhere, anytime."

"I doubt you will find it lurking hereabouts."

"Who knows?" he replied.

That evening, Kalifriki was awakened by strains of a wild music, faint in the distance. After a time, he struggled to his feet and out into the corridor. The sounds were coming up from the stairwell. Leaning against the wall, he listened for a long while, then limped back to bed.

The following day, after breakfast, he expressed his desire for a longer walk, and Yolara dismissed Dr. Shang and led Kalifriki down the stairs. Only gradually did he come to understand the enormous size of the building through which they moved.

"Yes," she commented when he remarked upon this. "It is built upon the ruins of an ancient abbey, and over the years it has served as fortress as well as residence."

"Fascinating," he said. "Tell me, I thought that I heard music last night. Was there some sort of celebration?"

"You might call it that," she answered. "My father left his rooms for the first time in a long while, and he summoned his musicians to play for him."

"I am glad that he is feeling better," Kalifriki said. "It was an eerie and beautiful music. I would like to hear it again one day—and perhaps even be present when the musicians perform it."

"They are returned to their crypts, somewhere beneath the floor," she said. "But who knows?"

"They, too, are creations of your father?"

"I think so," she answered. "But I've never really seen them, so it is difficult to say."

They passed an aviary of bronze birds, peculiar blue patina upon their wings, warbling, trilling, crying kerrew and fanning their feathers like turquoise screens. Some of them sat upon iron perches, some on nests of copper. A few of the nests contained silver eggs, while some held tiny birds, unfledged, beaks open to receive flies of foil, worms of tin. The air blurred and flashed about the singers when they moved.

In a garden in a southern courtyard she showed him a silver tree, bearing gleaming replicas of every sort of fruit he had ever seen and many he had not.

Passing up a corridor, Yolara halted before what Kalifriki at first took to be a portrait of herself, wearing a low-cut gown of black satin, a large emerald pendant in the shape of a ship riding the swells of her breasts. But upon closer regard the woman seemed more mature.

"My mother," Yolara said.

"Lovely," Kalifriki replied, "also."

At the end of the corridor was a red metal top as large as himself, spinning with a sad note, balanced upon the point of a dagger. Yolara told him that the top would rotate for ninety-nine years undisturbed.

She stated this so seriously that Kalifriki chuckled.

"I have not heard you laugh nor seen you smile," he said, "the entire time I've been here."

"These things are not fresh to me as they are to you," she replied. "I see them every day."

He nodded.

"Of course," he said.

Then she smiled. She squeezed his hand with a surprisingly firm grip.

The following day they went riding great horned horses of metal—he, mounted upon a purple stallion; she, a green mare. They sat for a long while on a hilltop, regarding the valley, the mountains, and the fortress of Jerobee Clockman. He told her somewhat of himself and her fascination seemed genuine, well beyond the point of courtesy. She seemed awkward when he finally kissed her, and it was not until the slow ride back that she told him she knew no humans other than her father, having met only an occasional merchant, minstrel, or messenger for brief spans of time.

"That seems a very odd way to live," he commented.

"Really?" she replied, "I was beginning to suspect this from reading books in the library. But since they are fiction to begin with, I could never be certain what parts were real."

"Your father seems like a peculiar man," said Kalifriki. "I would like to meet him."

"I am not sure he is entirely recovered," she said. "He has been avoiding me somewhat." Riding farther, she added, "I *would* like to see more of the world than this place."

That night when Kalifriki heard the music again he made his way slowly and quietly down the stairs. He paused just outside the hall from which the skirls and wailings flowed. Carefully, then, he lowered himself to his belly and inched forward, so that he could peer around the corner of the entranceway, his eyes but a few centimeters above the floor.

He beheld a metallic quartet with the blasted forms and visages of fallen angels. They were all of them crippled, their gray, gold, and silver bodies scorched, faces pocked, brows antlered or simply horned. Broken bat wings hung like black gossamer from their shoulders. There were two fiddlers, one piper, and one who performed on a rack of crystal bells. The music was stirring, chaotic, mesmerizing, yet somehow cold as a north wind on a winter's night. It was hardly human music, and Kalifriki found himself wondering whether the metal demons composed their own tunes. Behind them, in the floor, were five grave-sized openings, the four surrounding the fifth. Seated before them in a large, dark leather chair was a white-haired fat man whose features Kalifriki could not see, for the man had steepled his fingers and held them before his face. This did, however, draw his attention to a large sapphire ring upon the man's right hand.

When the piece was ended the creatures grew still. The man rose to his feet and took hold of a slim, red lance leaning against the nearest wall. Taking several steps forward, he struck its butt upon a crescent-shaped flagstone. Immediately, the musicians swivelled in place, approached their crypts, and descended into them. When they were below the level of the floor, stone covers slid into place, concealing all traces of their existence.

The man placed the lance upon a pair of pegs on the wall to his left, then crossed the room and went out of a door at its far end. Cautiously, Kalifriki rose, entered, and moved through. At the far door, he saw the form of the man reach the end of a hallway and begin mounting a stair, which he knew from an earlier walk to lead to the building's highest tower. He waited for a long while before taking down the lance. When he struck its butt against the curved stone, the floor opened and he stared down into the crypts.

The demon musicians emerged and stood, raising their instruments, preparing to play. But Kalifriki had already seen all that he cared to. He struck the stone once more and the quartet retired again. He restored the lance to its pegs and departed the hall.

For a long time he wandered the dim corridors, lost in thought. When, at length, he passed a lighted room and saw it to be a library with Dr. Shong seated within, reading, he paused.

"Kalifriki," said the doctor, "what is the matter?"

"I think better when I pace."

"You are still recovering and sleep will serve you more than thought."

"That is not how I am built. When I am troubled I pace and think."

"I was not aware of this engineering peculiarity. Tell me your trouble and perhaps I can help you."

"I have not met my host. Is Jerobee Clockman aware of my presence here?"

"Yes. I report to him every day."

"Oh. Has he any special orders concerning me?"

"To treat your injury, to feed you, and to see that you are extended every courtesy."

"Has he no desire to meet me in person?"

The doctor nodded.

"Yes, but I must remind you that he has not been well himself of late. He is sufficiently improved now, however, that he will be inviting you to dine with him tomorrow."

"Is it true that Yolara's mother ran off with a musician?" Kalifriki asked.

"So I have heard. I was not present in those days. I was created after Yolanda was grown."

"Thank you, Doctor," Kalifriki said, "and good night."

He limped on up to the hallway. When he turned the corner the limp vanished. Farther along the corridor he seated himself upon a bench, rolled up his trouser leg, and removed the elaborate brace he wore. Slowly, he rose to his feet. Then he shifted his weight. Then he smiled.

*

Later that evening Yolara heard a scratching upon her door.

"Who is it?" she asked.

"Kalifriki. I want to talk to you."

"A moment," she said.

She opened the door. He noted she was still fully clothed in the garments she had worn that day.

"How did you know which door was mine?" she asked him.

"I stepped outside and looked up," he replied. "This was the only room with a light on—apart from mine and the library, where I left Dr. Shong. And I know your father's rooms are in the North Tower."

She granted him her second smile.

"Ingenious," she stated. "What is it you wish to talk about?"

"First, a question—if I may."

"Surely." She stepped aside and held the door wide. "Please come in."

"Thank you."

He took the chair she offered him, then said, "When I awoke several days ago, Dr. Shong told me that I had been found at the scene of my accident three and a half days earlier."

She nodded.

"Were you present when I was discovered?"

"No," she answered. "I heard of you later."

"He used the pronoun 'we,' so I assumed that you were included. Do you know who else was with him?"

She shook her head.

"One of the other simulacra, most likely," she said. "But it might also have been my father. I think not, though, because of his illness."

"Yolara," he said, "something is wrong in this place. I feel that we are both in great danger. You have said that you would like to leave. Very well. Get some things together and I'll take you away, right now, tonight."

Her eyes widened.

"This is so abrupt! I would have to tell my father! I—"

"No!" he said. "He is the one I fear. I believe he is mad, Yolara—and very dangerous."

"He would never harm me," she said.

"I would not be too certain. You resemble your mother strongly, if that portrait be true. In his madness he may one day confuse you with her memory. Then you would be in danger."

Her eyes narrowed.

"You must tell me why you say this."

"I believe that he found your mother after her affair with the Gypsy, and that he killed her."

"How can you say that?"

"I've been to the hall where he keeps his demon quartet. I have opened their crypts—and a fifth one about which they assemble to play. In that fifth one is a skeleton. About its neck is the chain bearing the emerald ship which she is wearing in the painting."

"No! I do not believe it!"

"I am sorry."

"I must see this for myself."

"I would rather you did not."

"To make a charge like that and ask me to accept it on faith is too much," she stated. "Come! It would not be as bad as you may think, for my mother is a stranger to me. I would see this crypt."

"Very well."

He rose to his feet and they passed outside. Reaching into a shadowy alcove, he produced a length of bright steel, which he kept in his right hand as he led the way to the stairs.

"Where did you get the sword?" she asked.

"Borrowed it from a suit of armor downstairs."

"My father is a sick old man. It is hardly necessary to arm yourself against him."

"Then no harm is done," he replied.

"There is even more to this," she said, "isn't there?"

"We shall see," he answered.

When they came to the hall he had visited earlier, Kalifriki took the red lance down from the wall.

"Stand here," he directed, leading her to a place near to the middle crypt, and he stepped back and smote the crescent stone with the lance's butt.

The stones slid back and he hurried to her side. Her scream was not caused by the demons which rose to surround them, however. Looking down into the crypt, Kalifriki beheld the body of a fat, white-haired man whose head had been twisted around so that it faced completely to the rear. The body lay in the embrace of the ancient skeleton from whose neck the emerald ship depended.

"Who did this?" she asked.

"I don't know," Kalifriki said. "He was not there earlier. I don't understand. I—"

He knelt suddenly and reached down into the crypt. He raised the man's right hand.

"What is it?" she asked.

"A ring with a blue stone in it," he said. "He was wearing it earlier this evening. Now he is not."

"His signet," she said. "His seal as Master Toymaker. He would never part with it willingly."

Just then the demon quartet began to play and words became impossible. Lowering the toymaker's hand, Kalifriki picked up the red lance, which he had laid aside. He rose to his feet.

He passed between the crippled demons, and when he came to the crescent stone he struck it with the lance. Immediately, the music died. The performers retired to their crypts. The crypts began to close.

"Now do you at least believe that there is danger?" he said.

"Yes," she replied. "But—"

"Indeed there is," said the fat, white-haired man who entered through the far doorway, a flash of blue upon his right hand. "I heard your scream."

"Father's simulacrum," she said. "He'd often considered making one. I didn't know that he had. It's killed him and taken his place!"

The fat man smiled and advanced.

"Excellent," he said. "Hard to put one over on you, isn't it?"

"Where's its weakest spot?" Kalifriki asked her, raising the blade.

"Slightly below the navel," she answered, and he lowered the point of the weapon.

"Really," the simulacrum said, "beneath this guise of flesh you will find that you face metal against metal. It would take a good arm and a good blade to puncture me."

Kalifriki smiled.

"Shall we find out?" he asked.

The simulacrum halted.

"No, let's not," it replied. "It seems an awful waste of talent."

Its gaze moved past them then. Kalifriki turned his head, to see Dr. Shong enter through the other door.

"Doctor!" Yolara cried. "He's killed Father and taken his place!"

"I know," the ape replied, and she stared as he grinned. "He had an offer he couldn't refuse."

"My leg," Kalifriki said, "is not broken. I believe that it was, but it is healed now. That would have taken considerably longer than the few days you said it had been. I think I've been here for several weeks, that you've kept me drugged—"

"Very astute," Dr. Shong observed. "Also, correct. We had a special request of the late Jerobee Clockman. He did not finish the final adjustments until only a little while ago."

"And then you killed him!" Yolara cried.

"Just so," said the simian, nodding, "though his simulacrum did the actual physical business. But it is lèse majesté to call us killers in the presence of assassin royalty such as your guest. Isn't that right, Kalifriki?"

"Come closer, ape," he said.

"No. You seem to have figured out everything but why. So take the final step and tell me: What was Clockman's last creation—the thing he assembled that long while you slept?"

"I . . . I don't know," Kalifriki said.

"Come in!" Dr. Shong called out.

Kalifriki watched as his own double entered the room, a sword in its hand.

"Built according to your specifications," the ape stated. "Considerably stronger, though."

"I thought the Kife had fled."

His doppelganger bowed.

"You were incorrect," it told him.

Kalifriki slammed the butt of the lance against the crescent stone,

Yolara cried, "Killer!" and rushed toward the portly simulacrum, while the doppelganger advanced upon Kalifriki, the point of its blade describing a small circle in the air.

"By all means, let us dance," said his double, smiling, as the musicians took up their instruments and tuned them. The ape laughed, and Yolara cried out as she was thrown across the room to strike her head upon the hearthstone.

Snarling, Kalifriki turned away from his advancing double and, with a quick leap and an even quicker lunge, drove his blade into the simulacrum of Jerobee Clockman with such force that its point passed through its abdomen and protruded from its lower back. The weapon was wrenched from Kalifriki's grip as the figure suddenly raised both arms to shoulder height, extending them out to the sides, twisted its head into a bizarre position, and began the execution of a series of dance steps. With this, a small ratcheting noise commenced in the vicinity of its midsection.

Turning then, swinging the red lance in a circle, Kalifriki succeeded in parrying his double's attack. Retreating, the music swirling wildly about him, he ventured a glance at Yolara, discovering that she still had not moved. The glance almost cost him an ear, but he parried the thrust and riposted with a double-handed blow of the lance, which would have cracked a human's ribs but only slowed the simulacrum for a moment. During that movement, however, he struck it between the eyes with the butt of the weapon and, reversing it with a spin, jabbed for the abdomen with the lance's point. The attack was parried, though; and seeming to shake off all its effects, his doppelganger pressed him again. In the distance, he heard Dr. Shong chuckle.

Then he began to retreat once again, turning, passing behind the simulacrum of Jerobee Clockman—which was now dancing in extreme slow motion and emitting periodic clanging sounds. As it shifted its weight from left foot to right, he kicked it hard and it toppled in that direction, falling directly in the path of the double. Laughing, the doppelganger leaped over the twitching figure to continue its attack.

Kalifriki passed among the musicians then, dodging the fiddlers' bows, sidestepping to avoid collision with the bell rack. And his double came on, stamping, thrusting, parrying, and riposting. When he reached the position toward which he had been headed, Kalifriki pretended to stumble.

Predictably, the other attacked. Continuing his drop onto one knee and turning his body, Kalifriki executed a downward, rowing stroke with the lance, which caught the simulacrum behind the knees, sweeping it off balance. Springing to his feet then, Kalifriki struck it between the shoulder blades and rushed away as it toppled into the opened crypt. Slamming the butt of the lance against the crescent stone silenced the musicians immediately, and they tucked away their instruments, retreating toward their own crypts. Rushing among them, Kalifriki raised the lance once more to club down his doppeganger, should it try to emerge before the crypt sealed itself. It looked up and met his gaze.

"Fool!" it cried. "You guard me while the Kife flees!"

"Dr. Shong?" Kalifriki exclaimed, suddenly knowing it to be true.

Whirling, he hurled the lance at the running ape form, just as the crypt's lid slid shut above the simulacrum. The red shaft struck the hurrying figure's left shoulder with a terrific clang as it was about to cross the threshold of the nearer door. The impact turned it completely around. Miraculously, the ape did not fall, but teetered a moment, regained its balance, then rushed across the room toward the fireplace, left arm hanging useless.

Arriving before Kalifriki could take more than three paces, Dr. Shong knelt and reached, right hand fastening about Yolara's throat.

"Stop!" cried the ape. "I can decapitate her with a single movement! And I will if you come any nearer!"

Kalifriki halted, regarding the smear of blood on her temple.

"There was a time when I thought she might be a simulacrum," he said.

"I had toyed with the notion," said the other, "of replacing her with a version designed to kill you after you'd fallen in love with it. But I lack sufficient knowledge of human emotions. I was afraid it might take too long, or that it might not happen. Still, it would have been a delightful way of managing it."

Kalifriki nodded.

"What now?" he asked. "We seem stalemated here. Except that she does not appear to be breathing. If this is true, your threat is meaningless."

He began to take another step.

"Stop!" The Kife rose slowly, clasping her to its breast with forearm and elbow, its hand still at her throat. "I say she still lives. If you wish to gamble with her life, come ahead."

Kalifriki paused, his eyes narrowing. In the dim light, he saw the Thread upon the shoulder and waist of the simulacrum. Slowly, he raised his left arm. The Thread was also wrapped about his wrist. It extended back over his left shoulder. It extended forward. It joined with that segment of itself which hung upon the metal ape. It passed beyond, out of the door of the room. As Kalifriki flexed his fingers, it grew taut. As he continued the movement, the Kife turned its head, bewildered, as if looking for something in several directions. When Kalifriki closed his hand into a fist, the segments of Thread which had been looped about the Kife vanished from sight, slicing their ways into the metal body.

Moments later, the simulacrum collapsed, falling to the floor in three pieces. It had been decapitated and the torso separated from the legs at the waist. Yolara lay sprawled across its midsection, and its head rolled toward Kalifriki.

As Kalifriki stepped past it, it addressed him: "I lied. She is not breathing."

Kalifriki halted, picked up the head, and drew back his arm to hurl it against the nearest wall.

"But she may breathe again," it said, lips twisting into a smile, "if you but use your head."

"What do you mean?" Kalifriki asked. "Talk!"

"That which I stole from the Old Man of the Mountain—the Elixir of Life—it would revive her."

"Where is it?"

"I will tell you, in return for your promise that you will not destroy me."

Kalifriki turned the face away from his so that the Kife would not see him smile.

"Very well," he answered. "You have my word. Where is it?"

"Hidden among the gold and silver fruit in the bowl on the table beside the far door."

Kalifriki crossed the room, searched the bowl.

"Yes," he said at last, removing the small vial.

He unstoppered it and sniffed it. He placed his finger over the bottle's mouth, inverted it, returned it to an upright position. He placed upon his tongue the single droplet which clung to his fingertip.

"It is odorless and tasteless," he observed, "and I feel nothing. Are you certain this is not some trick?"

"Do not waste it, fool! It takes only a drop!"

"Very well. You had better be telling the truth."

He returned to Yolara's side and drew downward upon her chin to open her mouth. Then he removed another drop from the vial and placed it upon her tongue.

Moments later she drew a deep breath and sighed. Shortly thereafter, her eyelids fluttered and opened.

"What," she asked him, "has happened?"

"It is over," he said, raising her and holding her. "We live, and my job is finished."

"What was your job?" she inquired.

"To recover this vial," he explained, "and to bring back the head of its thief."

The brazen ape-head began to wail.

"You have tricked me!" it cried.

"You have tricked yourself," he replied, stoppering the bottle and pocketing it, helping Yolara to her feet.

"You are in charge here now," he told her. "If the memories are too bad for you, come with me and I will try to give you some better ones."

*

Now, as he led her through the Valley of Frozen Time, Kalifriki halted in a place that was sculpture, painting, map. He squeezed Yolara's arm and gestured at the incredible prospect which lay before them.

She smiled and nodded, just as the head of the Kife, which Kalifriki bore in his left hand, opened its mouth and bit him. He would have cursed, save that this was not a place of words (nor music, nor wind). He dropped the head, which rolled away, and he raised his hand to his mouth. The Kife's head fell into a crevice, where it rolled a considerable distance before coming to rest in precarious balance at the top of another incline, its position masked in darkest shadow. Search though he did, Kalifriki never found it, and had to settle for only half his pay, for the Old Man of Alamut is a harsh taskmaster. Still, this was not an inconsiderable amount, and with it he took Yolara on an amazing odyssey, to Byzantium, Venice, Cathay—but that is another story. The while, the Kife went mad of contemplating the turnings of fate; its brazen head fell from the ledge where it opened its jaw to scream, though this was not a place of screaming (nor music, nor wind); and it rolled the side—beside slopes down to a lane near Oxford, where a Franciscan named Roger Bacon found it. That, too, is another story. The Thread is always arriving and departing. It may wander anywhere and need not have an end.

COME BACK TO THE KILLING GROUND, ALICE, MY LOVE

1

All the death-traps in the galaxy, and she has to walk into mine. At first I didn't recognize her. And when I did I knew it still couldn't be right, her, there, with her blindfolded companion in the sandals and dark kimono. She was dead, the octad broken. There couldn't be another. Certain misgivings arose concerning this one. But I had no choice. Does one ever? There are things to do. Soon she will move. I will taste their spirits.

Play it again, Alices . . . .

2

She came to him at his villa in Constantinople, where, in loose-fitting garments, trowel in hand, spatulate knife at belt, he was kneeling amid flowers, tending one of his gardens A servant announced her arrival.

"Master, there is a lady at the gate," the old man told him, in Arabic.

"And who could that be?" the gardener mused, in the same tongue.

"She gave her name as Alyss," the servant replied, and added, "She speaks Greek with a foreign accent."

"Did you recognize the accent?"

"No. But she asked for you by name."

"I should hope so. One seldom calls on strangers for any good purpose."

"Not the Stassinopoulos name. She asked for Kalifriki."

33

"Oh, my. Business," he said, rising and passing the trowel to the man, dusting himself off. "It's been a long time."

"I suppose it has, Sir."

"Take her to the lesser courtyard, seat her in the shade, bring her tea, sherbet, melons—anything else she may desire. Tell her I'll be with her shortly."

"Yes, Sir."

Repairing within, the gardener removed his shirt and bathed quickly, closing his dark eyes as he splashed water over his high cheekbones then his chest, his arms. After drying, he bound his dark hair with a strip of golden cloth, located an embroidered white shirt with full sleeves within his wardrobe, donned it.

In the courtyard at a table beside the fountain, where a mosaic of dolphins sported beneath waters which trickled in small rivers from a man-sized Mt. Olympus, he bowed to the expressionless lady who had studied his approach. She rose slowly to her feet. Not tall, he observed, a full head shorter than himself, dark hair streaked with white, eyes very blue. A pale scar crossed her left cheek, vanished into the hair above her ear.

"Alyss, I believe?" he inquired, as she took his hand and raised it to her lips.

"Yes," she replied, lowering it. "Alice." She gave it a slightly different accenting than his man had done.

"That's all?"

"It is sufficient for my purposes, sir." He did not recognize her accent either, which annoyed him considerably.

He smiled and took the chair across from her as she reseated herself. He saw that her gaze was fixed upon the small star-shaped scar beside his right eye.

"Verifying a description?" he inquired as he poured himself a cup of tea.

"Would you be so kind as to let me see your left wrist?" she asked.

He shook back the sleeve. Her gaze fell almost greedily upon the red thread that was wrapped about it.

"You are the one," she said solemnly.

34

"Perhaps," he replied, sipping the tea. "You are younger than you would have your appearance indicate."

She nodded. "Older, also," she said.

"Have some of the sherbet," he invited, spooning two dishfuls from the bowl. "It's quite good."

3

I steady the dot. I touch the siphon and the bone. There, beyond the polished brass mirror, sipping something cool, her remarking in Greek that the day is warm, that it was good to find a shaded pausing place such as this caravanserai, my doorstep, in which to refresh themselves—this does not deceive me in its calculated nonchalance. When they have finished and risen, they will not head back to the street with its camels, dust, horses, cries of the vendors, I know that. They will turn, as if inadvertently, in the direction of this mirror. Her and the monk. Dead ladies, bear witness . . . .

4

"I can afford you," she told him, reaching for a soft leather bag on the flagging beside her chair.

"You precede yourself," he responded. "First I must understand what it is that you want of me."

She fixed him with her blue gaze and he felt the familiar chill of the nearness of death.

"You kill," she said simply, "Anything, if the price is right. That is what I was told."

He finished his tea, refilled their cups.

"I choose the jobs I will accept," he said. "I do not take on everything that is thrust at me."

"What considerations govern your choices?" she asked.

"I seldom slay the innocent," he replied, "by my definitions of innocence. Certain political situations might repel me—"

"An assassin with a conscience," she remarked.

"In a broad sense, yes."

"Anything else?"

"Madam, I am something of a last resort," he responded, "which is why my services are dear. Any simple cutthroat will suffice for much of what people want done in this area. I can recommend several competent individuals."

"In other words, you prefer the complicated ones, those offering a challenge to your skills?"

"'Prefer' is perhaps the wrong word. I am not certain what is the right one—at least in the Greek language. I do tend to find myself in such situations, though, as the higher-priced jobs seem to fall into that category, and those are normally the only ones I accept."

She smiled for the first time that morning, a small, bleak thing.

"It falls into that category," she said, "in that no one ever succeeded in such an undertaking as I require. As for innocence you will find none here. And the politics need be of no concern, for they are not of this world."

She nibbled a piece of melon.

"You have interested me," he said.

5

At last, they rise. The monk adjusts the small bow he bears and places his hand upon her shoulder. They cross the refreshment area. They are leaving! No! Could I have been wrong? I realize suddenly that I had wanted it to be her. That part of me I had thought fully absorbed and transformed is suddenly risen, seeks to command. I desire to cry out. Whether it be "Come!" or "Run!" I do not know. Yet neither matters. Not when it is not a part of her. Not when they are departing.

But.

At the threshold, she halts, saying something to her companion. I hear only the word "hair."

When she turns back there is a comb in her hand. She moves suddenly toward the dot manifestation which hangs brightly upon the wall to her right.

COME BACK TO THE KILLING GROUND, ALICE, MY LOVE

As she drops her veil and adjusts her red tresses I become aware that the color is unnatural.

6

"Not of this world," he repeated. "Whence, then, may I inquire?"

"Another planet, far across the galaxy from here," she replied. "Do these terms mean anything to you?"

"Yes," he answered. "Quite a bit. Why have you come?"

"Pursuit," she said.

"Of the one you would have me slay?"

"At first it was not destruction but rescue that we sought."

"'We'?"

"It took eight of me to power the devices which brought us here, an original and seven copies. Clones."

"I understand."

"Really? Are you, yourself, alien to this place?"

"Your story is the important one just now. You say there are eight of you about?"

She shook her head.

"I am the last," she stated. "The other seven perished in attempting the task I must complete."

"Which are you, the original or a clone?"

She laughed. Then, abruptly, her eyes were moist, and she turned away.

"I am a copy," she said, at length.

"And you still live," he remarked.

"It is not that I did not try, I went in after all of the others failed. I failed, too. I was badly injured. But I managed to escape—barely."

"How long ago was this?"

"Almost five years."

"A long time for a copy to stay alive."

"You know?"

"I know that many Cultures which employ clones for a particular job tend to build in some measure against their continued existence once the job is done, a kind of insurance against the . . . embarrassment . . . of the original."

"Or the replacement, yes. A small poison sac at the base of the skull in my case. I believe my head injury did something to nullify its operation."

She turned her head and raised her hair. There were more scars upon her neck.

"He thinks I am dead," she went on. "I am certain. Either from the encounter or from the passage of time. But I know the way in, and I learned something of the place's rules."

"I think you had better tell me about this person and this place," Kalifriki said.

7

The Alices are singing their wordless plaint. Now and forever. I build another wall, rings set within it, chains threaded through them. For all of them. Come back, come back, Alice, my last. It *is* you. It must be. Make the movement that will commit you, that will transport you. Else must I reach forth the siphon, as I have so many times. Even if it be not you, I must now. You resurrect an older self.

"Good," she says, putting away her comb, turning toward the door.
No!
Then she turns back, lips set in a tight line, raising her hand, touching the reflecting surface. A moment, as she locates the pulses, passes her hand through the activation sequence.

As her fingers penetrate the interface the bowman is suddenly behind her, laying his hand upon her shoulder. No matter. He may bear an interesting story within him.

8

"Aidon," she said. "He is Aidon."
"The one you seek?" Kalifriki asked. "The one you would have me kill?"

38

"Yes," she said. Then, "No. We must go to a special place," she finished.

"I don't understand," he said. "What place?"

"Aidon."

"Is Aidon the name of a man or the name of a place?"

"Both," she said. "Neither."

"I have studied with Zen masters and with Sufi sages," he said, "but I can make no sense of what you are saying. What is Aidon?"

"Aidon is an intelligent being. Aidon is also a place. Aidon is not entirely a man. Aidon is not such a place as places are in this world."

"Ah," he said. "Aidon is an artificial intelligence, a construct."

"Yes," she said. "No."

"I will stop asking questions," he stated, "for now. just tell me about Aidon."

She nodded once, sharply.

"When we came to this system looking for Nelsor," she began, "the ship's instruments showed that something on this planet had gained control of a cosmic string, circumnavigating the universe, present since its creation. We dismissed this at the time, for it was actually one of the tiny holes of blackness—an object supercollapsed to an unworldly point, also present since the creation—that we were seeking. For this would lead us to Nelsor's vessel, from which a damage-pulse had come to us. We use the black objects to power our way through other spaces. Do you understand?"

"That part, yes," he said. "I don't understand who or what Nelsor is, let alone Aidon."

"They are the same," she said, "now. Nelsor was her—the original Alice's—lover, mate, consort, husband-relation. He piloted the vessel which had the trouble, and they came down in this general area of your planet. I believe that Aidon took control of the vessel—and of Nelsor as well—and caused the landing here, and that this is what triggered the damage-pulse."

She glanced at him.

"Aidon," she said, "is difficult to explain. Aidon began as one of those small, black, collapsed objects which make a hole in space. We use them as specialized devices. Bypassing space for distant travel is one of the ends for which they are employed. They are set up for most of their jobs-travel included—by swirling a field of particles about them at high velocity. These fields are impressed with considerable data for the jobs they are to perform. The field is refreshed at its outer perimeter, and the data is replicated and transferred outward in waves as the inner perimeter is absorbed. So there is a matching informed particle-feed to equal the interior information loss. The device draws on the radiation from the collapsed object for power and is programmed to be self-regulating in this regard."

"I understand what you are saying," Kalifriki replied, "and possibly even where this is going now. Such a thing becomes intelligent-sentient?"

"Generally. And normally their input is well controlled," she answered.

"But not always?"

She smiled, momentarily. Kalifriki poured more tea.

"Of all categories of employment, there is less control over the input of those used in space travel," she responded, "and I suppose that the very act of traversing the peculiar domains they must has its odd results. The experts are not in agreement on this. One thing which definitely affects such a construct, however, is that for certain areas of space passage the pilot must maintain constant direct communication with it. This requires a special sort of person for pilot, one possessing the ability to reach it mentally—a telepathic individual with special training for working with constructed intelligences. Such a relationship will infect the construct to some extent with the operator's personality."

She paused for a drink of tea.

Then, "Sometimes such constructs become disordered, perhaps from staring too long into the heart of darkness between the stars. In a human we would call it madness The vessels often simply vanish when this happens. Other times, if it occurs in known space there may be a signature pulse indicating the vehicle's destruction. As with Aidon, they may digest their operators' minds first—an overlay that could enhance the madness to a kind of schizophrenia."

COME BACK TO THE KILLING GROUND, ALICE, MY LOVE

"So Aidon ate Nelsor," said Kalifriki, raising his cup, "and brought the vessel to Earth."

She nodded.

"Whatever had grown twisted within him twists whatever it acquires. It twisted Nelsor's feelings for Alice. He destroyed the four Alices one by one, so that he might know them in their pain. For this is how he learned love, as a kind of pain, from the twistings of darkness that damaged him, to the pain of Nelsor's passing. Not totally alien, perhaps, for there are people who love through pain, also."

Kalifriki nodded.

"But how do you know that this is the case with Aidon?" he asked.

"Alice was also a pilot," she said, "and as such, a sensitive. She had a strong bond of this sort with Nelsor. All of her clones shared her ability. When she brought the final three of us and came seeking him—for he seemed still alive, but somehow changed—this was the means by which we located the entrance to the blister universe he had created."

"He has his own world?"

"Yes. He formed it and retreated to it quickly after coming to this place. And there he dwells, like a trapdoor spider. Alice entered and was destroyed by him. We all felt it happen. Then, one by one, the three of us who remained essayed the passage—each succeeding in penetrating a little farther into the place because of her predecessor's experience. But each of the others was destroyed in the process. I was the last, so I knew the most of how his world operated. It is a kind of slow killing machine, a torture device. I was injured but was able to escape."

She brushed at her scar.

"What could you have hoped to accomplish?" he asked. "Why did you keep going in when you saw what he was up to?"

"We hoped to reach a point where we could communicate with that part of him which is still Nelsor. Then, by linking minds, we had thought to be able to strengthen him to overcome Aidon. We hoped that we could save him."

"I thought he was dead–physically, that is."

"Yes, but in that place, with that power, he would have been godlike, if he could have been freed even briefly and gained control of Aidon again. He might have been able to reconstitute his body and come away in it,"

"But . . ." Kalifriki said.

"Yes. Aidon proved so much stronger than what remained of Nelsor that I saw it could never be. There is no choice now but to destroy Aidon."

"Why not just let him be if he's retreated to his own universe?"

"I can hear their cries–Nelsor's, and those of the ravished souls of my sisters. There must be some release for what remains of them all. And there are others now. The entrance to his underworld lies hidden in a public house on a trade route. When a sufficiently sensitive individual enters there, Aidon becomes aware of it, and he takes that person to him. He has developed a taste for life stories along with his pain He extracts them both, in a kind of slow feasting. But there is more. You are aware of the nature of such objects. You must realize that one day he will destroy this world. He leeches off it. Eventually, he will absorb it all. It will hover forever in a jumble of images on his event horizon, but it will be gone."

"You would hire me to destroy a black hole?"

"I would hire you to destroy Aidon."

Kalifriki rose and paced through several turns.

"There are many problems," he said at last.

"Yes," she replied, drinking her tea.

9

. . . Passing through the mirror into my world, hand emerging from a lake, slim white arm upthrust as if holding the sword in that story the Frenchman had. And hesitation. Coy, her return, as if waiting for me to reach out, to hand her through. Perhaps I shall. There is amusement to be had in this. Come, siphon . . . .

Fading, faded, gone. The arm. She wavered and went out, like a flame in a sudden draft. Gone from beneath the lake, behind the mirror. Along with the blind monk. To what realm transported? Gone from the inn, from my world, also.

But wait . . . .

10

"You are asking me to pit my thread, in some way, against a singularity," he said,

"How is it that your string resembles a piece of red thread?" she asked.

"I require a visible appearance for it locally," he said, "to have something to work with. I do not like your idea."

"As I understand these things, your thread goes all the way around the universe. It was this that we detected on our approach. There are fundamental physical reasons why it can never have an end. A singularity could not bite a piece out of it. The antigravity of its pressure would exactly cancel the gravity of the energy. So there would be no net change in the gravity of the black hole which tried to take it in. The hole would not grow in size, and the situation would remain static in that regard. But you would have Aidon hooked with the string passing through him. Could you then transfer him to another universe?"

Kalifriki shook his head.

"No matter what I might do with him that way, the hole would remain permanently attached to the thread, and that is unacceptable. It might cause unusual loopings. No. I will not match two such fundamental objects directly against each other. If I am to be retained to destroy Aidon I will do it my way, Alice. Aidon, as I understand it, is not really the black hole itself, but a self sustaining, programmed accretion disc which has suffered irreparable damage to its information field. That could be the point of my attack."

"I don't see how you would proceed with it."

"I see only one way, but it would mean that you would not be able to return to your home world."

She laughed.

"I came here prepared to die in this enterprise," she said. "But, since the black hole cannot be destroyed and you will not attempt shifting it to another universe, I need to know what your attack will involve—as further disruption of the information will involve Nelsor as well as Aidon."

"Oh? You said you'd given up on Nelsor, that what was left of him was ruined and merged with Aidon, that that only course remaining was to destroy the entire construct."

"Yes, but your talk of my not returning home implied that you wanted my ship or something from it. That could only be its singularity drive."

"You're right."

"So you intend somehow to use one black hole against the other. And it could work. Such a sudden increase in mass without a compensating acceleration of the field could result in its absorbing the field faster than the field could replicate itself. You would make the hole eat Aidon and Nelsor both."

"Correct."

"I don't see how you could get close enough to do it. But that is, as you say, your problem. I might be able to penetrate Aidon's world to a point where I could communicate with Nelsor mentally and make a final effort to save him, to complete my mission. I want you to hold off on doing what you contemplate until I've tried."

"That would narrow our safety margin considerably. Why this sudden change of heart?"

"It was because I saw the possibility when I began to understand your plan. Bringing another singularity into that place might perturb Aidon to the point where he may lose some control over what he holds of Nelsor. if there is any chance he might still be freed . . . I must try, though I be but an image of his lady. Also, my telepathic bond with him may be stronger than that of any of the other six."

"Why is that?" Kalifriki asked.

She reddened and looked away. She raised her cup and lowered it again without drinking.

COME BACK TO THE KILLING GROUND, ALICE, MY LOVE

"Nelsor took no sexual pleasure with the clones," she said, "only with the original Alice. One time, however, I was in her quarters seeking some navigational notes we had discussed while she was occupied in another part of the vessel. He came seeking her and mistook me for his lady. He had been working hard and I felt sorry for him in his need for release. So I assumed her role and let him use me as he would her, giving him what pleasure I could. We enjoyed each other, and he whispered endearments and later he went away to work again. It was never discovered, and I've never spoken of it till now. But I have heard that such things can strengthen the bond."

"So you care for him in a somewhat different way than the others," Kalifriki said, "as he did for you, whatever the circumstances."

"Yes," she replied, "for I am her equal in all ways, not just genetically, having known him as the other six did not."

"So you would undertake an even greater risk for him?"

"I would."

"And if you fail?"

"I'd still want you to destroy him, for mercy's sake."

"And if you succeed, and the world is coming apart about us? It may be harder to escape under those circumstances. I don't really know."

She reached for her bag.

"I brought all the gold bars I could carry comfortably. There are a great many more aboard my vessel. "I'll give them all to you—"

"Where is your vessel?"

"Beneath the Sea of Marmara, I could summon it, but it were better to go out in a boat and simply raise it for a time."

"Let me see how much gold you have in the sack."

She hefted it and passed it to him.

"You're stronger than you look," he said as he accepted it. He opened it then and examined its contents. "Good," he said. "But we will need more than this."

"I told you you can have it all. We can go and get it now."

"It would not be for me, but for the purchase of equipment," he told her. "This bag and another like it should suffice for that, if I take the job."

"There will still be ample metal left for your fee," she said. "Much more than this. You will take the job, won't You?"

"Yes, I will."

She was on her feet.

"I will get you the gold now. When can we leave for Ubar?"

"Ubar? That is where Aidon has opened his office?"

"Yes. It lies near an Arabian trade route."

"I know the place. We cannot go there immediately, however. First, there are preparations to be made."

"Who are you really?" she asked him. "You know too much. More than the culture of this world contains."

"My story is not part of the bargain," he said. "You may rest now. My servant will show you to a suite. Dine with me this evening. There are more details that I wish to know concerning Aidon's world. Tomorrow I would inspect your vessel and obtain the additional gold we will need for a trip we must take."

"Not to Ubar?"

"To India, where I would obtain a certain diamond of which I have heard, of a certain perfection and a certain shape."

"That will be a long journey."

"Not really. Not as I shall conduct it."

"By some employment of the string? You can do that?" He nodded. "How did you gain such control over a thing like that?"

"As you said, Alice, I know too much."

11

. . . But wait. Now they are back. Her arm still extends above the waters of my lake. Likely but some trick of the interface, some roving particle's hit within the nanocircuitry, that fogged the transfer. They come now into my world, wet white garment clinging to the well-remembered contours of her

46

form—nipples above their orbs, curves of hip and back and buttocks, shoulders, thighs—ripe for the delicate raking of claws. And the man, he is more muscular than first I thought. A lover, then, perhaps. Then to see those muscles flex when the skin has been removed to the waist . . . there is that to fill the air with the music of outcry and weeping. Dead Alices, give them a song as they come ashore, of welcome to their new home, through crystal forest beneath a sky of perfect blue. How long from that then to this now? Centuries. As entropy here rockets to the sharp curves of my architecture, the contours of its form rake of my desire. The arrow of time passes and returns down sharp geodesics, pierces memory to the rage, impales rage that the love may flow. Why did you come back, form of hatred and its opposite? You will tell me, upon the ground I have prepared for you, tell, to the chorus of your sisters beneath a bleeding sky. But we must not rush these things, Alice, my last. For when you are done the ages will be long, the glory of your exposed architecture a piece of frozen time, distributed in monument about the crying landscape. Come back to the Killing Ground, Alice, my love. I've many a present to gift you there, the entire universe our angel of record against the long dark time. Set foot upon the shore and find your way. The ladies sing your nuptials in the Place of Facing Skulls.

12

Kalifriki dropped the anchor and struck the sails of their boat, as Alice moved to the bow and began singing in a lilting language he did not understand. The beginning morning's light touched the waves with flecks of gold and a cool breeze stirred her zebra hair upon her shoulder. He leaned against the gunwale and watched her as he listened. After a time the boat rose with a long, slow swell, subsiding only gradually. Her voice went out across the water, vibrated within it, and suddenly her eyes widened, reminding him of one of the Acropolis Maidens, as the water roiled to starboard and a curving, burnished form surfaced there like the back of some great, mysterious sea creature rising to meet the day.

He stirred himself, fetching a pole with a hook affixed to its end to grapple them closer to the bronzed surfaces. He glanced back at her before he used it, and she nodded. Reaching then, he caught it within one of the stair-like projections which had rippled into being upon its side, leading up to a hatch. He drew them nearer until he felt the scraping of their hull upon metal.

"Grown, not fabricated," he remarked.

"Yes," she replied, moving forward.

He held the grapple until she had crossed over to the alien vessel's companionway. Then he set it aside and followed.

By the time he came up behind her she had the hatch open. She entered and he looked down into a lighted interior, down to a soft green deck which might be covered with tailored grasses, furniture built into niches in contoured walls without corners.

Entering, he descended. Barely visible scenes flashed across surfaces he passed. A small vibration communicated itself to him, through the floor, through the air. They passed rooms both bright and muted, traversing corridors with windows that seemed to open upon alien landscapes—one, where red, treelike forms scrambled across an ebony landscape beneath a double sun causing him to pause and stare, as if remembering.

At length, she halted before a tan bulkhead, manipulated a hatch set within it, flung it open. Stack upon stack of small golden bars lay within the revealed compartment, gleaming as through a hint of green haze.

"Take all you want," she said.

"I want another bag such as the first, for the transaction of which I spoke," he told her, "and another after that for the first half of my fee. I will claim the final payment when the job is done. But we can collect these on the way out. I wish to view the source of the ship's power now."

"Come this way."

He followed her farther into the vessel's interior, coming at last to a circular chamber where watery visions appeared around the walls, including one of the underside of his boat, off to his right.

"This is the place," Alice said.

COME BACK TO THE KILLING GROUND, ALICE, MY LOVE

Kalifriki did not see what she did, but suddenly the floor became transparent and far beneath his feet it seemed that something pulsed darkly. There came a dizziness and he felt drawn toward the center of the room.

"Open it," he said.

"Move back two paces, first."

He obeyed. Then the floor opened before him, the section where he had been standing dropping to become three steps leading down to a narrow well. Its forward wall housed a clear compartment within which he seemed to feel the presence of something drawing him. He descended the steps,

"What are the dangers? What are the safeguards?" he asked.

"You are safe where you are," she answered. "I can open the panel and give you a closer look."

"Go ahead."

It slid back and he stared for a moment.

"How would you manipulate it?" he asked.

"Forcefield pressures against its container," she replied.

He shook out a strand of the thread from his wrist, snaked it about the opening several times, withdrawing it slowly on each occasion.

"All right, I can work with this," he said a little later. "Seal it in again."

The compartment closed before him.

" . . . Pure carbon crystal lattice, antigrav field webbed throughout," he said as to himself. "Yes. I saw something like this managed once, a long time ago." He turned and mounted the stair. "Let's go in and get the gold. Then we can head back."

They withdrew the way they had come in, returning to the boat with two heavy sacks. The vessel's hatch secured, she sang it back beneath the waves. The sun stood now fully risen, and birds dipped toward the waters about them as he weighed the anchor and set the sails.

"Now?" she said.

"Breakfast," he replied.

"Then?" she asked.

"India," he said.

49

THE NIGHT KINGS AND NIGHT HEIRS

13

Now the monk has fully entered my world, following her. Suddenly, things are no longer as they have been. Things are no longer right. Things seem to collapse like strange wave functions about him as he passes. Yet nothing seems really changed. What has he brought with him into my world, that I feel uneasy at his presence here? Is it a kind of turbulence? Is it that I am running faster? It would be hard to tell if my spin state were affected. Where did she find him? Why did she bring him? An aged tree reaches the end of its growth and shatters as he goes by it. I do not believe I like this man, shuffling unseeing through my gardens of crystal and stone. Yet perhaps I shall like him a great deal when the time comes. Such feelings are often close akin. In the meantime, it is always amusing to observe when a new thing comes to this place. My *arbor decapitant* awaits, but fifty paces ahead. She knows of it, of course. All of the Alices learned of it, the first the hard way. Yet it is good sport to see such things do their business. Yes, he will be all right. New blood must be brought to the game from time to time, else there is no bite to it. I will let them play through, to the end of her knowledge . . . .

14

In Maharajah Alamkara's palace of white marble they were feasted and entertained with music and dance, for Kalifriki had once done some work for that ruler involving a phantom tiger and some missing members of the royal family. Late into the evening a storyteller regaled them with an almost unrecognizable version of the event.

The following day, as Kalifriki and Alice walked amid walls of roses in the royal gardens, the chamberlain, Rasa, sent for them to discuss the business to which Kalifriki had alluded the previous evening.

Seated across the counting table from the heavy dark man of the curled and shiny mustaches, they beheld the stone known as the Dagger of Rama, displayed on a folded black cloth before them. Almost four inches in length, it was broad at the base, tapering upward to a sharp apex; its outline would be that of a somewhat elongated isosceles triangle, save that the lower corners were missing. It was perfectly clear, without a hint of color to it. Kalifriki raised it, breathed upon it. The condensation of his breath vanished immediately. He scrutinized it then through a glass.

"A perfect stone," Rasa said. "You will find no flaws."

Kalifriki continued his examination.

"It may hold up long enough," he said to Alice in Greek, "if I frame it appropriately, using certain properties of the thread to control external considerations."

"A most lovely stone for your lady to wear between her breasts," Rasa continued. "It is sure to influence the *chakra* of the heart." He smiled then.

Kalifriki placed a bag of gold upon the table, opened it, poured forth its contents.

Rasa picked up one of the small bars and studied it. He scratched it with his dagger's point and measured it, turban bobbing above the gauge. Then he placed it upon a scale he had set up to his left and took its weight.

"Of great purity," he remarked, tossing it back upon the table. Then he raised several of the bars from the pile and let them fall from his hand. "Still, it is not enough for so remarkable a stone. It may well have accompanied Rama on his journey to confront Ravan in the matter of Sita's abduction."

"I am not interested in its history," Kalifriki replied, and he brought up the second bag of gold and added its bars to the heap. "I've heard report that the tax collectors have had a lean time these past several years."

"Lies!" Rasa stated, opening a nearby chest and dipping his hand into it. He withdrew and cast forth a fistful of semiprecious stones upon the tabletop. Among them lay a small carved mountain of pale green jade, a pathway winding about it in a clockwise direction from base to summit. His gaze falling upon this piece, he reached out and tapped it with a thick forefinger. "Sooner would this spiral change direction," he said, "than would I undersell a treasure simply to raise funds."

Kalifriki raised his wrist. The thread touched upon the piece of jade, seemed to pass within it. The stone moved slightly. The spiral now wound in the opposite direction.

Rasa's eyes widened.

"I had forgotten," he said softly, "that you are the magician who slew the phantom tiger."

"I didn't really kill him," Kalifriki said. "He's still out there somewhere. I just came to terms with him. Storytellers don't know everything."

The man sighed and touched his middle.

"This job is sometimes very trying," he said, "and sometimes seems to give me pains in my stomach. Excuse me."

He removed a small vial from a pouch at his sash, as Kalifriki moved his wrist again. As he unstoppered the container and raised it to his lips, Kalifriki said, "Wait."

Rasa lowered the vial.

"Yes?" he asked.

"If I heal your ulcer," Kalifriki said, "you may well bring it back with too much worry and aggravate it with too many spices. Do you understand?"

"Heal it," he said. "It is hard to cultivate philosophy in the face of necessity, and I do like my foods well seasoned. But I will try."

Kalifriki moved his wrist again and Rasa smiled. He stoppered the vial and replaced it in the pouch.

"All right, magician," he said. "Leave the gold. Take the stone. And if you see the white tiger again, let it know that you pass this way occasionally and that bargains are to be kept."

Later, in the garden at twilight, Alice asked him, "How did you do that reversal on the stone?"

"The full circumference of the thread is less than 360 degrees," Kalifriki replied. "The negative pressure of antigravity affects the geometry of space about it. Its missing angle is my key to other spaces. I simply rotated the stone through a higher space."

She nodded.

"I seem to recall something of this property from my training," she said. "But how did you heal the ulcer?"

"I speeded up time in its vicinity, letting the natural processes of his body heal it. I hope that he takes my advice and learns some detachment, from his work and his food."

They took a further turn, into an area of the garden they had not yet explored. The Bowers seemed to grow flat upon a flattening prospect along the twisting trail they followed. Then they were gone and it was the dead of night with great winnowings of stars blazing above them as they entered the lesser courtyard of Kalifriki's villa at Constantinople.

"You still smell of roses," she said.

"So do you," he replied, "and good night.

15

. . . Walking through my forest, ridiculous archaic weapon upon his back, his hand upon her shoulder, the monk follows the Alice. This one, I note, is scarred. My last Alice, then. She did escape, of course. And gone all this time. Planning, surely. What might she have in mind for the final foray, the last gasp of the octad? Its aim, certainly, is to free Nelsor. Nelsor . . . Even now, I feel her reaching out toward him. Disturbing. She is the strongest in this regard. Yet soon she will be distracted. They approach my favorite tree. Soon now . . . It spins in its socket, each limb a saber of glass. But she drops to the ground at precisely the right moment, and her monk moves with her in instant response. They inch their way forward now, the limbs flashing harmlessly, cold fire above them. Yet Endway's Shoot is next, where I took my second Alice, and the Passage of Moons may take them yet, even aware of the peril. And already she calls again. Nelsor . . . ?

16

Kalifriki sat all the next day in meditation, his bow before him upon the ground. When he had finished he walked on the shore for a long while, watching the waves come in.

Alice met him on his return and they took a late supper together.

"When do you plan to embark for Ubar?" she asked him, after a long silent time.

"Soon," he said, "if all goes well."

"We will visit my vessel in the morning?"

"Yes."

"And then?"

"It depends partly on how long the work there takes."

"Partly?"

"I think that I will want to meditate some more afterwards. I do not know how long that will take."

"Whenever . . . " she answered.

"I know that you are eager," he said later. "But this part must not be rushed."

"I understand."

He walked with her then into the town, passing lighted residences, some shops, government buildings. Many of the sounds of the city had grown still with the darkness, but there was music from some establishments, shouts, laughter, the creaking of a few passing carts, the stamping of horses' feet; they smelled spices in some neighborhoods, perfumes in others, incense from a church.

"What did you do," he asked her, from across a table where they sat sipping a sharp yellow wine, "in the five years between your escape from Aidon and your coming to see me?"

"I traveled," she replied, "seeking you—or someone like you—and trying to find the surface locus of that string. It had seemed bound to this world, as if it were somehow being employed. I supposed that one who had mastered it could be the one I needed to help me in this. I traveled with many servants—with some large male always in charge—as if I were part of a great man's retinue rather than owner of the lot, It is difficult being a woman on this world. I visited Egypt, Athens, Rome, many places. Finally, I heard stories of a man called Kalifriki, who had been employed by Popes,

Emperors, Sultans. I traced the stories down. It took a long time, but I could afford to pay for every scrap of information. They led me here."

"Who told you the stories?"

"A poet. He called himself Omar, tentmaker."

"Ah, yes. A good man. Drank too much, though," said Kalifriki, sipping his wine. "And locally?"

"A priest named Basileos."

"Yes. One of my agents. I am surprised he did not warn me."

"I came immediately. I hurried. There was no opportunity for him to beat my arrival with a message. He told me to make further inquiry of Stassinopoulos, but I decided to ask for you here by name instead. I suspected by then that you had a second identity, and I was certain that a man such as yourself would be too curious not to give me audience under the circumstances. I was in a hurry. Five years of hearing their cries has been too long."

"You still hear them, right now?"

"No. Tonight they are silent," she said.

The moon fell down the sky, was caught in the Golden Horn.

17

Now, Nelsor, they have reached the Shoot, a mountain hurtling by them, but feet above the ground. They must crawl upon their bellies here, and even then, if one of my small satellites whose long ellipse brings it by here has so rotated that some downward projection rakes the land—*quish!* A pair of stepped-on cockroaches. Too fast? True. But this is but the foreplay, dear companion, my mentor. She calls to you again. Do you hear her? Do you wish to answer her? Can you? Ah! another rock and a jagged beauty it is!—races its purple shadow above the blood-red way. By them. And still they crawl. No matter. There will be more.

THE NIGHT KINGS AND NIGHT HEIRS

18

They completed the transfer on the Sea of Marmara that morning and afternoon. Then Kalifriki, clad in brown kimono and sandals, meditated for a brief time. At some point his hand went forward to take hold of the bow. Bearing it with him, he walked away from his villa down toward the sea. Alice, glimpsing his passage from her window, followed him at a distance. She saw him walk upon the shore, then halt, take forth a cloth and bind his eyes with it. He braced the bow, removed an arrow from its case, set it against the string. Then he stood holding them, unmoving.

Minutes passed on toward the end of day and he did not stir. A gull flew near, screaming. The better part of an hour went by. Then another gull passed. Kalifriki raised the bow almost casually, drew it, released the arrow into the air. It passed beside the bird and a single feather came loose, drifted downward.

He removed the cloth from his eyes and watched the feather rock its way to the water. She wanted to sing, but she only smiled.

Kalifriki turned then and waved to her.

"We leave for Ubar in the morning," he called out.

"Did you want the bird or the feather?" she asked, as they walked toward each other.

"To eat the bird is not to digest its flight," he replied.

19

They have passed Endway's Shoot, where my moons flow like a string of bright beads. Leaving the passage like a trail of blood behind them, they rise, turning sharply to the left, climbing to the yellow ridge that will take them down into the valley where they must pass through my Garden of Frozen Beings, the place where I collected my third Alice . . . . What is that? A question? A chuckle?

Nelsor? Do you stir? Would you enjoy a ticket to this final festival? Why, then you shall have one, if you be able to use it, I have not felt such enthusiasm from you in ages. Come then to me if you can. I touch the bone, you I summon you, lord, my mentor, to this place and time, Nelsor, for you were always my master in the matter of killing Alices. It is fitting that you be present when the collection is made complete. Come to me now, Nelsor, out of darkness. This spectacle is yours. By bone, siphon, and clot, I summon you! Come!

20

They came to Ubar, city of Shaddad ibn Ad, to be called Iram in the Koran, oasis town of lofty pillars, "the like of which were not produced in the land." Alice's hair was red now, and she wore a white garment and a light veil upon her face; Kalifriki had on his kimono and sandals, a cloth about his eyes, his bow upon his back, lacquered case beside it containing a single arrow.

Passing amid a sea of tents, they made their way down avenues lined with merchants, traders, beggars, to the sound of camel bells, gusts of wind, and the rattle of palm fronds. Conversation, song, and invective sounded about them in a double-dozen tongues. They came at last to the great gated pillars through which they passed, entering into the town proper, where the splashing sounds of fountains came to them from within adobe walled gardens; and white-stuccoed buildings gleamed in the morning sun, bands of blue, green, red, and yellow tiles adorning their palace-high walls.

"I seem to recall the dining area of the inn as being located in a kind of grotto," Kalifriki said, "within a rocky hillside, with the rest of the establishment constructed right, left, and forward of it, using the face of the hillside as a rear wall."

"That is correct," she said. "The cavern keeps the place cool by day. The cooking fires are well vented to the rear. You descend four or five stone steps on entering, bearing to the right—"

"Where is the mirror located?"

"On the wall to the left as you go in, below the steps."

"Metal, isn't it?"

"Brass or bronze—I forget."

"Then let us go in, be seated, have a cooling drink, and make certain that everything is still this way. On the way out, pause and investigate the mirror as you pretend to study your appearance. Lower the veil as you do so. If it attempts to draw you through, I will be near enough for you to take my hand. if it does not, turn away as if you are about to depart. Then return, as in afterthought, and employ that transport sequence you learned from your predecessors."

"Yes. There is the place up ahead now," she said.

He followed, and she took him in.

21

See, Nelsor? They are at the Garden of Frozen Beings now, place of your own design, if you recall—though in your original plan it was only for display. I came across it in an odd memory cache. See how Cunningly it is wrought? It holds your studies of living things from a dozen worlds, in all sizes and colors, set upon many levels, in many interesting poses. Impossible not to pass it on several at any given time. I added the Series Perilous.

I took an Alice here, Crushed by the blue spiral, eighth from the left—where she lay long in two pieces, gasping—for not calculating the death sequence correctly; and one back at Endway's Shoot, smeared to a long streak, though barely noticeable upon the red-stone, and another well flayed and diced in the crystal forest, by my *arbor decapitant.*

The first three, which you managed yourself—before your second disorientation—were so much more elegantly done . . . .

22

Finishing their drinks, Kalifriki and Alice rose and crossed the refreshment area. They passed the metal mirror and mounted the steps. At the threshold, she paused.

"A moment," she said. "I want to check my hair in that mirror we passed."

Returning down the stair, she produced a comb. At the mirror, she made a quick adjustment of several stray tresses, letting her veil fall as she did so.

COME BACK TO THE KILLING GROUND, ALICE, MY LOVE

Kalifriki stood behind her. "We must be at least partway entered before I shift." he whispered, "if I am to lay the thread in that universe so as to benefit our course through it. Remember what I said of the phenomenon. Whenever you are ready . . . "

"Good," she said, putting away her comb, turning toward the door.

Three beats later she turned back, lips set in a tight line, raising her hand, touching upon the reflecting surface. After a moment she located the pulses, passed her hand through the activation sequence.

As her fingers penetrated the interface, Kalifriki, behind her, placed his hand upon her shoulder, following a small squeeze from her free hand.

Her entire arm passed through the interface, and Kalifriki took them to the Valley of Frozen Time, where he removed his blindfold. He regarded the thread's passage through the placeless time into the timeless place, its twistings were complicated, the nexuses of menace manifold. Alice tried to speak to him, not knowing that words, like wind or music, could not manifest in this place of sculpture, painting, map. Twisting the thread, he flicked it three times, to see it settle at last into the most appropriate bessel functions he could manage under the circumstances, racing ahead to meet himself down thoroughfares of worlds-yet-to-be, and even as it plied its bright way he felt the tug of Time Thawing, replaced his blindfold, and set his hand again upon Alice's shoulder, to feel them drawn back to the waters of a small lake in the toy universe of the collector of Alices, piecemeal, who must even now be wondering at their interrupted passage.

23

Good of you to have summoned me back to my world, Aidon. What have you done to it? What are these silly games you have been about? Aidon, Aidon . . . Is this how you read my intention? Did you really think the bitches worth the concerted efforts of an entire universe, to crush them in manners you found esthetically gratify? Did you think I wanted to construct a theme amusement park? You profane the memory of the woman I love. You should have taken instruction from my disposition of the first three.

59

There was a point to those—a very important point. One which you have been neglecting.

Lord, Nelsor, master, my mentor. I am sorry if the program is faulty. I had it that the killing of Alices was the highest value in the universe, as taken from your own example. See! See how this one must scramble, to avoid the hanging twar? *She has generalized the experience of two of her sisters, to learn it is not the* twar *nor the* twar's *physical position that matters, but rather that position in the sequence of encounters. She had to abstract the series from the previous deaths. See how she must scramble—and her companion after her—to dodge the falling* frogbart, *leap high above the lower limb of the* gride? *When the* bropples *rolled around them she knew just how to dive—and to stand perfectly still till the* wonjit *exhausted its energies. See where the* jankel *has cut her arm? And even now she must pass the way of the* vum. *There is fine sport in her gasping, her bleeding, the tearing of her garments in seeing the sweat pour from her. And the* slyth *yet remains, and the* fangrace-pair. *Tell me how this differs from the doomed races where you ran the earlier Alices. How have I mistaken your intent? When you ceased being able to, function I was proud to take on your role. I am sorry if—*

Aidon, it broke me to do as I did with the first three. I retreated into my second madness over my actions, still unsatisfied worse than unsatisfied, actually. I hated them, true, and it made it easier to do what I had to, to learn certain things. Still, it hurt me, also, especially in that I did not learn what I wished, though it narrowed the field. You should have summoned me for the fourth, the fifth, the sixth. There was data that I required there—lost to me now!

Not so, lord! For I recorded them! You can summon them! Have them back! Deal with them further I have done it many times—for practice. I even bring in outsiders for fresh rites. I have performed the ritual of the dying Alices over and over in your name—hoping to effect your repair in the reenactment. I have been faithful to your procedure—What? You have not employed that command mode since ship-time . . . . You would retire me? Do not! There is an important thing I have yet to tell you! I—

COME BACK TO THE KILLING GROUND, ALICE, MY LOVE

Go away, Aidon. Go away. I would rid myself of your bumbling presence, for you have offended me. Let us say that it was an honest mistake. Still, I no longer wish to have you about, chortling over my undertakings, misreading all my actions, distracting me with your apologies. Before you fade entirely, see how I dismantle your remaining stations of blood. It is not games that *I* desire of the scarred lady I hate. But you are right in one thing. I will have the others back, as you recorded them, messy though the prospect be. She will follow the thread of a new course to the Place of Facing Skulls. By dot, bone, and siphon, this one will give me what I want. Go away, Aidon. Go away

Come back to the Killing Ground, Alice, my last. The rules you've learned no longer apply. Keep calling to me. You shall have my answer, a piece at a time.

24

Provoking the *fangrace-pair* to attack simultaneously, Alice left them tangled in each other's many limbs. Passing behind the nearer then, she led Kalifriki to a narrow bridge which took them above a canyon whose bottom was lost in blackness. Achieving its farther side, she took him down a twisting way beneath an evening sky of dark blue wherein lights that were not stars burned unblinking at near distances. Vivid, against the darkness, an incandescent rainbow took form.

"Strange," she muttered.

"What?" Kalifriki asked.

"There was never a rainbow here before."

"And it is night, is it not?" Kalifriki asked.

"Yes. It began darkening as we entered that last place."

"In some traditions on Earth a rainbow is the sign of a new covenant," Kalifriki said.

"If that is the message, it is more cryptic than communicative," she said.

Suddenly, the faint sounds of female voices which had been with them constantly since their arrival rose in volume. From sighs to wailings, they had been shaped somehow into a slow, eerie tune which rose and fell as if working toward an ominous crescendo it never quite reached, returning constantly to begin again, yet another variation on plaints of pain, punctuated with staccato bursts of hysterical laughter.

A cool wind came by, gusting among the high rocks amid which they moved. On several occasions, the ground shook beneath their feet.

Reaching the end of their downward way and turning to the left, Alice beheld a deep crater in which a lake of orange lava boiled, flames darting above it, casting its light upon the high, piped walls which Surrounded it. Their trail split here, an arm of it going, in either direction about the lake's oval perimeter, cinder-strewn between its jagged shores and the rise of the organpipe walls.

Alice halted.

"What is the matter?" Kalifriki asked.

"A burning lake," she said. "It wasn't here before."

"What was?"

"A maze, full of pits and deadfalls, flooded periodically with rushing torrents,"

"What now?"

"I suppose we must choose a way and go on, to find the place of which I told you that first night over dinner—the place we have glimpsed but never quite reached. There are bones there, and an open wall. I think it is the place of the singularity. Which way should I go?"

"Let us trust to the falling of the thread. Find a random way to choose."

She stooped and picked up a pebble. Turning, she cast it, hard, back in the direction from which they had come. It struck against the rock wall and bounded back. It rolled past them to the right.

"Right," she said, and they turned and took up their way again, in that direction.

The trail was perhaps six feet in width, light from the blazing cauldron to their left casting their shadows grotesquely upon the fluted wall. The way curved in and out as they went; and they felt the heat-painfully, after a time-upon their left sides. Dark fumes obscured the starlike lights in the sky, though the rainbow still glowed brightly. The chorus of pained voices was partly muted by the popping and crackling from below, by the faint roaring that came in undertone.

As they rounded a bend they heard a moaning.

"Alice . . . " came a soft call from the right.

She halted.

Bleeding from countless cuts, one leg missing from below the knee, the other from above it, left arm dangling by a thread of flesh, a woman who resembled her lay upon a low ledge to the right, face twisted in the orange glow, her remaining eye focused upon them.

"Alice—don't—go—on," she gasped. "It—is—awful. Kill me—quickly—please . . . ."

"What happened? What did this to you?" Alice asked.

"The tree—tree of glass—by the lake."

"But that is far. How did you get here?"

"Don't know," came the reply. "Why is it—so? What have we done?"

"I don't know."

"Kill me."

"I cannot."

"Please . . . ."

Kalifriki moved forward. Alice did not see what he did. But she knew, and the broken lady did not call to them again.

They passed on in silence then, the lake growing more turbulent as they moved, now shooting great fountains of fire and molten material high into the air. The heat and fumes grew more oppressive. Periodically, niches glowed again in the wall to their right, wherein bleeding Alices stood, eyes staring, unseeing, straight ahead, lips twisting in their song which rose in intensity now, overcoming the lake's roaring. Whenever they approached these figures, however, they faded, though the song remained.

Then, in the flaring light, as they neared the far end of the trail, Alice beheld a rough area amid the cinders and congealed slag. She slowed, as she realized that the mangled remains of a human body were smeared before her, still somehow stirring. She halted when she saw the half-crushed head beside the way.

Its lips moved, and a wavery voice said, "Give him what he wants, that I may know peace."

"What—What is it that he wants?" she asked.

"You know," it gasped. "You know. Tell him!"

Then the lake bubbled and roared more loudly. A great strand of flame and lava leaped above it and fell toward them. Alice retreated quickly, pushing Kalifriki backward behind her. The fiery mass fell across the trail, obliterating the remains, draining, fuming, back into the lake. When it was gone, the ground smoking before them, the remains of the dead Alice had vanished, also.

They halted, waiting for the way to cool, and Kalifriki asked, "What is this knowledge of which she spoke?"

"I—I'm not certain," Alice replied.

"I've a feeling," Kalifriki said, "the question will be repeated in more specific and equally colorful terms at some point."

"I'd guess you're right," she told him.

Shortly, they walked on, treading quickly across the ravaged area, beneath the rainbow, the song suddenly reaching a higher pitch of wailing as they went.

As they neared the farther end of the lake, another molten spume reached near at hand. Alice halted, waiting to see in which direction the flashing tower might topple. But it stood, swaying, for a long while, almost as if trying to decide the matter itself it took on a spiraling twist for a while before abruptly falling toward the wall perhaps twenty paces ahead of them.

They retreated even farther as this occurred. The spume fell in slow motion above the trail, its tip touching the wall, whence it flowed downward to the right hand trail's edge. Its upper portion remained in place, ten or twelve feet overhead, spirals working through it in two directions, braiding themselves now into a sputtering yellow-orange fretwork of light and molten material. The archway thus formed ceased its swaying and stood pulsing before them.

"We suddenly have a burning gate ahead of us," Alice stated.

"Is there any other way to proceed?" Kalifriki asked.

"No," she said.

"Then it would seem we have little choice."

"True. I just wanted you to know the nature of this encounter."

"Thank you. I am ready."

They moved ahead, and the archway maintained its position as they approached. Passing beneath it, the air was filled with crackling sounds and the prospect wavered. Alice's next step took her onto a rough silvery way with nothing about her but the starlike lights. Another pace, and Kalifriki had passed through also, the gateway vanishing behind him.

It was not a continuous surface upon which they stood, but rather a forty-foot span of about the same width as the trail they had quitted. It ended abruptly in all directions. Looking downward over its edge, she saw, at a distance impossible to estimate, the twisted surface of the land they had been traversing, cracked, pierced, brightly pied, monoliths darting about its surface, the rainbow still arched above it; and even as she watched, it seemed to change shape, lakes flowing into valleys, flames leaping up out of shadows and crests, new jigsaw pieces of color replacing old ones with less than perfect fit. And about them, still, rang the plaints of the dead Alices. She moved ahead, toward the farther end of the silver way.

"We're high above the land," she said, "walking on the surface of a narrow asteroid. It is like a broken-out piece of a bridge. I'm heading toward its farther end."

"Alice," Kalifriki said as they began to move again, "I have a question."

"What is it?"

"Did you come to Earth on the first vessel or the second?"

"Why do you ask that?"

"You said that Nelsor and four clones came here and had their trouble. Then later, his Alice, learning of this, made the voyage with the three remaining clones, yourself among them."

"Did I? I don't recall exactly how I phrased it."

"Then, when you told me of your bedroom encounter with Nelsor, it sounded as if you, he, and the original Alice all made a single journey together."

"Oh. That happened on a different voyage, elsewhere."

"I see," Kalifriki said, matching her pace.

Tenuous wisps of fog swept by them as they walked, followed by larger puffs. Something massive drifted downward from overhead, possibly on a collision course, possibly about to miss them. It was of about the same shape and albedo as the thing on which they moved.

"Another asteroid headed this way," she reported. "A bit of fog's come by, too."

"Let's keep going to the end."

"Yes."

Just as they reached the extremity of their way, the second piece of spanning slid into place before them and remained there, as if joined with their own. This one curved to the left.

"We've acquired an extension," she said. "I'm going to continue along it."

"Do so."

Several additional pieces moved by as they walked—one of them the section they had quitted, removing itself from the rear and drifting forward to join them again ahead.

"It's extending itself down toward a cloud bank," she told him, as she peered in the new direction it was taking. Then, too, they seemed to be moving, relative to the overall form of the shifting panorama below.

She crossed to another section. The clouds came on quickly, they were of soft pink, pale blue, light lime, streaked through each other in delicate abstract waves.

Several hundred paces later she heard a scream. Halting, and looking to the right, whence it seemed to have come, she beheld nothing but clouds. She began to gnaw at her lower lip as the cry was repeated.

"What is it?" Kalifriki asked.

"I don't know."

COME BACK TO THE KILLING GROUND, ALICE, MY LOVE

Then the clouds parted, and she saw a pair of drifting boulders but a few feet distant. The upper torso, head, and shoulders of a woman resembling herself lay sprawled upon the left-hand stone. Severed from these and occupying the slightly lower right-hand one lay the rest of her, twitching.

"Alice!" the figure cried. "He would know which of us was responsible. None of us could tell him. That leaves only you. Tell him what happened, for mercy's sake!"

Then the two rocks flew off in opposite directions and the clouds closed in again. Kalifriki could feel Alice shaking.

"If you know whatever it is he wants," he said, "perhaps you should tell him. It may make life a lot easier."

"Perhaps I do and perhaps I don't," she said. "I suppose I'll learn when I'm asked a direct question. Oh!"

"What? What is it?"

"Nelsor. I reached him for a moment. Or he reached me. He is gone now."

"Could you tell anything about his condition?"

"He seemed a mix of emotions. Happy that I was coming—in some other way disturbed. I don't know."

They walked again. The singing went on, and periodically they could feel the vibrations as new pieces of their twisted passageway through the sky assembled themselves. The colored fogs parted and came together again, flirting with her vision, providing tantalizing glimpses of some vantage that lay far ahead.

Their way seemed telescoped from break to break in their passage through the fog. Suddenly, Alice halted, stiffening, saying "Stop!" sharply.

"What is it?" Kalifriki asked.

"End of the trail, for the moment," she replied. "It just stops here. We are at the edge, and I am looking down again, through a thinning fog, at the distant land. The fog at our sides is dissipating now, too. That which is ahead of us is still thick. A redness flows through it."

They waited, and the red mist passed by degrees, revealing, first, an almost sculpted-seeming rocky prominence, pointed centrally, descending

67

symmetrically at either hand and curving forward into a pair of gray-blue stony shoulders, and before them a flat yellow oval of sandy stone, raised above lesser steplike formations, irregular, more blue than gray, descending into mist. To the rear, set within the bulk of the prominence, a shelf-like niche was recessed at shoulder height; and at the oval's approximate center lay a well, a low wall of red stone blocks about its mouth. Another structured wall—this one of black stone—stood to the far left and downward of the oval, perhaps twenty feet in length, eight in height. Chains hung upon it. And this entire vision seemed to be quivering, as through a heat-haze.

More of the mist blew away, and the lines of the lower slopes came into view. Watching, as the last of it fled, Alice saw that the base of the entire prominence was an abruptly terminated thing, at about twice the height's distance below the oval, jagged blue icicles hanging beneath, as if a frozen mountaintop had been torn loose and hurled into space to hover against the blackness and the unblinking points of light; and now she could see that the rainbow's end lay within the oval.

Despite this clearing, the entire monumental affair still seemed to be vibrating.

"What is it?" Kalifriki asked at last.

Slowly, she began describing it to him.

25

Nelsor, I had only one thing to tell you before, but now I have two. Please acknowledge. There is perturbation within the well of the dot because another singularity is approaching—also a second peculiar item, of energy and negative field pressure trapped within a tube. Please acknowledge. This is a serious matter. I understand now what it was about the monk which first troubled me. Here at the center of things I can feel it clearly. He is very dangerous and should be removed from our universe at once. Release me and I will deal with him immediately Acknowledge, Nelsor! Acknowledge! There is danger here!

COME BACK TO THE KILLING GROUND, ALICE, MY LOVE

Oh. The other thing I wanted to tell you concerns the first Alice. I had located some small memory caches for her. They were inadvertently recorded because of a peculiar conflict situation. Nelsor, I am going to begin pushing against this retirement program if you do not answer me . . . .

26

Alice stared at the vibrating landscape in the sky. A final span of bridge came drifting in slowly from her right, streaming colors as it passed through the rainbow. The voices of her dead sisters ceased, and only the wind that blows between the worlds could be heard in its chill passage.

"It is called the Killing Ground," she said then. "It has been transferred here from another location since my last visit. It is the final place."

"You never referred to it so before," Kalifriki said.

"I only just learned the name. I have reached Nelsor again. Or he has reached me. He bids me cross over. He says, 'Come back to the Killing Ground, Alice, my last.'"

"I thought you had never been to the final place."

"I told you I had glimpsed it."

As the last piece of bridge slid into place, connecting their span with the lowest step beneath the oval, she saw the vibrations shake loose a small white object from the niche. With a Sudden clarity of vision, she discerned it to be a skull. It bounced, then rolled, coming to rest in the sand near a spreading red stain.

"Kalifriki," she said, "I am afraid. He is changed. Everything is chanced. I don't want to cross over to that place."

"I don't believe I can get us out at this point," Kalifriki said. "I feel we are bound too tightly to my initial disposition of the thread, back in the Valley of Frozen Time, to employ it otherwise here. We must pass through whatever lies ahead, or be stopped by it."

"Please make certain," she asked, licking her lips. "He is calling again . . . .

27

Alice, Alice, Alice. You must be the one. It could have been none of the other wasted ladies. Even if Aidon fumbled in his approach by not putting the questions, there should have been some lapse on their part, some betrayal of the truth, should there not? The guilty one would not even have come in . . . . Why, why are you here at all? And that stranger at your side . . . . What is your plan? If it is you, why are you here? I am troubled. I must put you the questions. Why did you come back, Alice my last? It must be you . . . mustn't it? And why do you hesitate now? Come back to the Killing Ground, where her blood stains the sand and our skills lie in constant testimony to the crime Come back. No? Then I call upon the siphon to bear you to me, here in the last place, beside the well of the dot that is the center of the universe. Even now it snakes forth. You *will* come to me, Alice, here and now, on this most holy ground of truth. I reach for you. You cannot resist Not now, Aidon.

Not now. Go back. Go back. I have retired you. Go back.

It comes for you, Alice.

28

"I am sorry," Kalifriki said. "It is as I told you."

Staring ahead, Alice saw a black line emerge from the well, lash about, grow still, then move again, rising, swaying in her direction, lengthening . . . .

"The siphon," she said. "A piece of ship's equipment. Very versatile. He is sending it—for me."

"Is it better to wait for it or go on?"

"I would rather walk than be dragged. Perhaps he will not employ it if I come on my own."

She began moving again. The black hose, which had been approaching, snakelike, halted its advance as she came toward it down the final length of silver. When she came up in front of it, it retreated. Step by step then, it withdrew before her. She hesitated a moment when she came to the end of the span. It leaned slightly toward her. At this, she took another step. It backed off immediately.

COME BACK TO THE KILLING GROUND, ALICE, MY LOVE

"We're here," she said to Kalifriki. "There are several ledges now, like a rough stairway, to climb."

She began mounting them, and as soon as she reached the flat sandy area the siphon withdrew entirely, back into the well. She continued to advance, looking about. She came to the well, halted, and peered down into it.

"We are at the well," she said, and Kalifriki removed his hand from her shoulder and reached down to feel along its wall. "It goes all the way through this—asteroid," she continued. "The dot—the black hole—is down there at its center. The siphon is coiled about the inner perimeter, near to the lip. It shrinks, so that one circuit is sufficient to house it. Below, I can see the bright swirling of the disc. It is far down inside—perhaps midway."

"So this place is being eaten, down at its center," Kalifriki said. "I wonder if that is the cause of the vibration

She walked on, past the red stain and the skull, to regard the niche from which the skull had tumbled. Another skull rested there, far to the right, and a collection of pincers, tongs, drills, hammers, and chains lay in the middle area.

"Torture tools here," she observed.

Kalifriki, in the meantime, was pacing about the area, touching everything he encountered. Finally, he stopped beside the well. Looking back, Alice saw that the rainbow fell upon his shoulders.

Then, above the sighing of the wind, there came a voice.

"I am going to kill you, Alice," it said. "Very slowly and very terribly."

"Why?" she asked.

The voice seemed to be coming from the vicinity of the skull. It was, as she recalled it, the voice of Nelsor.

"All of the others are dead," he said. Now it is your turn. Why did you come back?"

"I came here to help you," she said, "if I could."

"Why?" he asked, and the skull turned over so that the empty sockets faced her.

"Because I love you," she replied.

There came a dry chuckling sound.

"How kind of you," he said then. "Let us have a musical accompaniment to that tender sentiment. Alices, Give us a song."

Immediately, the awful plaint began again, this time from near at hand. To her right, six nude duplicates of herself suddenly hung in chains upon the black wall. They were bruised but unmutilated. Their eyes did not focus upon any particular objects as they began to shriek and wait. At the end of their line hung a final set of chains.

"When I have done with you, you shall join my chorus," Nelsor's voice went on,

"Done?" she said, raising a pair of pliers from the ledge and replacing it. "Employing things such as this?"

"Of course," he replied.

"I love you, Nelsor."

"That should make it all the more interesting."

"You are mad."

"I don't deny it."

"Could you forget all this and let me help you?"

"Forget? Never. I am in control here. And it is not your love or your help that I seek."

She looked at Kalifriki, and he removed the bow from his shoulder and strung it. Then he opened the case and withdrew its arrow, the spectrum blazing upon its tip.

"If your friend wishes to punch a hole in my head, that is all right with me. It will not let out the evil spirits, though."

"Is it possible for you to reembody yourself and come away with me?" she asked.

Again, the laugh.

"I shall not leave this place, and neither shall you," he said.

Kalifriki set the arrow to the bowstring.

"Not now, Aidon!" Nelsor shouted. Then, "Or perhaps your friend would shoot an arrow down the well to destroy the dot?" he said. "if he can, by all means bid him do so. For destroying the universe is the only thing I know to protect you from my wrath."

"You heard him, Kalifriki," she said.

Kalifriki drew back upon the bowstring.

"You are a fool," Nelsor said, "to bring—of all things—an archer here to destroy me . . . one of the legendary ones, I gather, who need not even see the target . . . against a dead man and a black hole."

Kalifriki turned suddenly, leaning back, arrow pointed somewhere overhead.

" . . . And a disoriented one, at that," he added.

Kalifriki held this position, his body vibrating in time with the ground.

"You are a doomed, perverse fool," Nelsor said, "and I will use your sisters in your questioning through pain, in testament against you. They will rend you, stretch you, dislocate you, crack your bones."

There came a sound of chains rattling against stone. The chorus was diminished by half as the restraints fell from three of the Alices and their singing ceased. At that moment, their eyes focused upon her, and they began to move forward.

"Let it begin," he said, "in this place of bloody truth."

Kalifriki released his arrow, upward. Bearing its dark burden, the Dagger of Rama sped high and vanished into the blackness.

29

Nelsor! She has brought with her a being capable of destroying our universe, and it is possible that he just has. I must perform some massive calculations to confirm my suspicion—but in the meantime our survival depends upon our acting as if it is correct. We cannot return to our alpha point and start again if I am destroyed. And if I am destroyed you are destroyed, along with this place and all of your Alices. We are facing the end of the world! I must confer with you immediately!

THE NIGHT KINGS AND NIGHT HEIRS

30

The three Alices advanced upon the first stair.

31

Aidon! Whatever it is, this is not the time for it! I am finally arrived at the moment for which I have waited all these years. I find your importunities distracting. Whatever it is, deal with it yourself, as you would. I will not be interrupted till I have done with this Alice. Stay away from me until then!

32

The three Alices mounted the first step. At their back, their sisters' song reached a new pitch, as if the crescendo might finally be attained.

33

Very well, Nelsor. I shall act. First Alice, I summon what remains of you. By bone, dot, and siphon, I call you to embodiment upon the Killing Ground! Perhaps you can reason with him.

34

Alice glanced at her three sisters, approaching now upon the farther stair. Kalifriki lowered his bow and unbraced it, slung it. He reached up then and removed the bandage from his eyes.

"Nelsor, listen to me," Alice said. "Aidon will be destroyed. So will the programs which maintain your own existence—unless you reembody and shift your entire consciousness back into human form. Do that and come away with me, for this place is doomed. No matter what our differences, we can resolve them and be happy again. I will take good care of you."

"'Again'?" Nelsor said. "When were we ever subject to mutual happiness? I do not understand you, clone. What I do not understand most, however, is why one of you killed my wife. And I feel strongly that it was you, Alice my last. Would you care to comment on this?"

From somewhere, a bell began to ring.

COME BACK TO THE KILLING GROUND, ALICE, MY LOVE

"Who sounds the ship's alert?" he cried.

"Probably Aidon," she responded, "as it realizes the truth of what I have been saying."

"You have not yet answered my question," he said. "Did you kill my wife?"

The second skull fell from the niche, rolled to the bloody area near to the first. The bell continued to ring. The voices of the three chained Alices rose and rose.

She grimaced. The other Alices mounted another step.

"It was self-defense," she said. "She attacked me. I had no desire to harm her."

"Why would she attack you?"

"She was jealous—of us."

"What? How could that be? There was nothing between us,"

"But there was," she said. "You once mistook me for her, and we had our pleasure of it."

"Why did you permit it?"

"For you," she said. "I wanted to comfort you in your need. I love you."

"Then it could have gone by and been forgotten. How did she learn of it?"

"I told her, when she singled me out for reprimand over something one of the others had done. She slapped me and I slapped her back. Soon we were fighting on the ground, here—when this place was elsewhere. She struck me about the head with a tool she had at her belt. This is why I wear these scars. I thought she would kill me. But there was a rock nearby. I raised it and swung it. I was not trying to kill her, only to save myself."

"So you are the one."

"We are the same. You know that. Down to the cellular level. Down to the genes. You cannot have her back. Have me instead, I am the same flesh. You could not tell the difference then. it will feel the same now. And I will be better to you than she ever was. She was rude, imperious, egotistical. Come back. Come away with me, Nelsor my love. I will care for you always."

He screamed, and the three Alices halted at the top of the stair.

Slowly, a haze formed about the skull which faced her.

"Go back, Alices. Go back," he said. "I will deal with her myself."

The skull fell backward—now somewhat more than a skull, as the outlines of features had occurred about it in the haze—and a wavering began beneath it, delineating the form of a body, pulsing it into greater definition. Beside it, however, a similar phenomenon began to invest the second skull. The three Alices at the edge of the oval turned away, began walking back down the stair just as their sisters hit and ran the crescendo, voices changing from wailing to pure song, The three never returned to the wall, however, but faded from sight before they reached the bottom stair. At that time, the chains rang against the wall, and Kalifriki saw that the others had vanished as well.

Shortly, the nude form of a dark-haired, short-bearded man of medium stature took shape, breathing slowly, upon the sand. Beside him, another Alice came into focus, grew more and more substantial.

"You did not tell me the full story," Kalifriki said as they watched.

"I told you everything essential to the job. Would more detail have changed anything?"

"Perhaps," he said. "You fled after the fight, and this is your first time back then, correct?"

"Yes," she said.

"So you were not party to the other six Alices' journeys to this place, save that you monitored them to learn what you could of it."

"That's right."

"You might have warned them that any of them would be suspect. And after the first of them died you knew Nelsor's state of mind. You let your sisters go to their deaths without trying to stop them."

She looked away.

"It would have done no good," she said. "They were determined to resolve the matter. And you must remember that they were monitoring, too. After the first death, they were as aware as I was of his state of mind, and of the danger."

"Why didn't you stop the first one?"

"I was . . . weak," she said. "I was afraid. It would have meant telling them my story. They might have restrained me, to send me home for trial."

"You wished to take the place of the first Alice."

"I can't deny it."

"I suppose that is her upon the ground now."

"Who else could it be?"

Nelsor and the new Alice opened their eyes at about the same time.

"Is it you?" Nelsor asked softly.

"Yes," she answered.

Nelsor raised himself onto his elbows, sat up.

"So long . . . " he said. "It has been so long."

She smiled and sat up. In a moment they were in each other's arms. When they parted and she spoke again, her words were slurred:

"Aidon—message for you—to me gave," she said.

He rose to his feet, helped her to hers.

"What is the matter?" he asked.

"'Portant, 'im, to talk to. World ending. Arrow."

"It is nothing," Nelsor said. "He shot it off in the wrong direction. What is wrong with you?"

"Cur-va-ture. Perfect vector," she said, "to cir-cum-navi-gate small our uni-verse. Back soon. Other way."

"It doesn't matter," he said. "It's just an arrow."

She shook her head.

"It bears—an-other—dot."

"What? It's carrying a singularity around the universe on a collision course with Aidon?"

She nodded.

He turned away from her, to face Kalifriki.

"This is true?" he asked.

"This is true," Kalifriki replied.

"I don't believe it."

"Wait awhile," he said.

"It still won't destroy Aidon."

"Perhaps not, but it will destroy the programmed accretion disc and probably wreck your world that it holds together. "

"What did she pay you to do this?"

"A lot," he said. "I don't kill for nothing if I can help it."

"The conscience of a mercenary," Nelsor said.

"I never killed three women who were trying to help me—for nothing."

"You don't understand."

"No. Is that because we're all aliens? Or is it something else?"

Just then, the new-risen Alice screamed. Both men turned their heads. She had wandered to the niche where her skull had lain, and only then seemed to notice her scarred clone standing nearby.

"You!" she cried. "Hurt me!"

She snatched the hammer from the ledge and rushed toward the clone. The Alice dodged her assault, reached for her wrist and missed, then pushed her away.

"She's damaged," Nelsor said, moving forward. "She's not responsible . . . "

The original Alice recovered and continued her attack as Nelsor rushed toward them. Again, the other dodged and pushed, struck, pushed again. The incomplete Alice staggered backward, recovered her footing, screamed, swung the hammer again as her double moved to close with her.

Nelsor was almost upon them, when a final push carried her backward to strike her calves against the lip of the well.

He was wellside in an instant, reaching, reaching, leaning, and catching hold of her wrist. He continued to lean, was bent forward, fell. He disappeared into the well with her, their cries echoing back for several seconds, then ceasing abruptly.

"Lost!" the remaining Alice cried. "She has taken him from me!"

Kalifriki moved to the edge of the well and looked downward.

"Another case of self-defense," he said, "against the woman you wished to replace."

"Woman?" she said, moving forward. "She was incomplete, barely human. And you saw her attack me."

He nodded.

"Was it Nelsor you really wanted?" he said. "Or this? To be the last, the only, the mistress—the original?"

Tears ran down her cheeks.

"No, I loved him," she said.

"The feeling, apparently, was not mutual."

"You're wrong!" she said. "He did care!"

"As a clone. Not as his woman, Give up the memory. You are your own person now. Come! We should be leaving. I don't know exactly when—"

"No!" she cried, and the ground shook and the chains rattled. "No! I am mistress here now, and I will reembody him without memory of her! I will summon the three recorded clones to serve us. The others were witless. We shall dwell here together and make of it a new world. We can bring in what we choose, create what we need—"

"It is too late for that," Kalifriki said. "You brought me here to destroy a universe and I did. Even if it could be saved, you cannot dwell on the Killing Ground forever. It is already destroying you. Come away now, Find a new life—"

"No!" she answered. "I rule here! Even now, I take control of Aidon! I remember the command modes! I have reached him! I hold this universe in my hand! I can alter the very physical constants! I can warp space itself to turn your silly arrow away! Behold! I have digested its flight!"

The lights in the sky flickered for the first time and jumped to new positions.

"Change the topology and the geodesic will follow,"

Kalifriki said. "The Dagger of Rama will still find you. Come away!"

"You! You have hated me all along for what I am! As soon as I told you I was a clone you knew I was something less than the rest of you! But I can destroy you now, assassin! For I am mistress of the dot! I can wish you away in any manner I choose! There is no defense!"

"So it comes to that again," he said. "You would have me pit my thread against a singularity."

She laughed wildly.

"There is no contest there," she said. "You have already described the entanglement that would result. I believe I will burn you—"

Kalifriki moved his wrist, slowly, to a position above the well.

"What are you doing?" she said. "How can you interfere with my omniscience? My omnipotence? You can't touch me!"

"I told you that the circumference of the thread is less than a full circle," he stated. "I am cutting out a wedge from your disc."

"That close? You can't. If the warp extends to the hole you would violate thermodynamics. A black hole cannot shrink."

"No," he said. "The thread would probably be caused to deliver energy to replace it and increase the mass and the radius in compensation. But I am being careful not to let it stray so near, and not to have to test this hypothesis. My sense is extended along it."

"Then you will not die by fire," she said, slurring her words slightly. "By bone—dot—and siphon—I summon you! Sisters! Destroy this man!"

Kalifriki's head jerked to the left, the direction of her gaze.

The three Alices whose eyes focused were flickering into existence across the oval from him. Slowly, he withdrew his wrist beyond the well's wall.

"Kill him!" she said. "Before he kills us! Hurry!"

The three Alices moved, wraithlike, even before they were fully embodied, rainbow's light passing through them as they came on.

Solidifying before they arrived, they rushed past Kalifriki, to attack the one who had summoned them.

"Murderess!" one of them cried.

"Liar!" shrieked another.

"Cause of all our pain!" screamed the third.

The scarred Alice retreated, and Kalifriki shook out his thread so that it fell among them. A wall of flame rose up between the Alices and their victim.

"There is no time," he called out, "to stain this ground further! We must depart!"

He moved the thread to enclose the three Alices.

"I am taking them with me," he said. "You come, too! We must go!"

"No!" she answered, eyes flashing. "I will shunt your arrow. I will move this place itself! I will warp space even more!" The lights in the sky winked again, danced again. "I will avoid your doom, archer! I will—rebuild! I will—have—him—back! I—am—mistress—here—now! Begone! I—banish—the—lot— of—you!"

Kalifriki retreated with the three ladies, to the Valley of Frozen Time. There, in the place that is sculpture, painting, map, he laid his way home He could not speak to explain this, for this was not a place for words (nor wind, music, cries, wailing), nor they to thank him, were that their wish. And while scarred Alice stood upon the Killing Ground and invoked the powers of dot, siphon, and bone against the rushing Dagger of Rama as it cut its way around the universe, Kalifriki transported the three Alices from the land behind the mirror in vanished Ubar, taking them with him to his villa near the sea, though he feared them, knowing that he could never favor one over the others. But that was a problem to be dealt with at another time, for the ways of the thread are full of arrivals and departures, and even its master cannot digest its flight fully.

35

Alice at the end of the rainbow stands upon the red stain and watches the sky. The siphon brings her nourishment as she plies powers against powers in her contest with the inexorable doom she has loosed. A darkhaired, short-bearded man of medium stature sits upon the edge of the well and seems to watch her. Occasionally, she takes her pleasure of him and he tells her whatever she wishes to hear. She returns, refreshed then, to her duel, though it sometimes feels as if the circle of her universe no longer possesses 360 degrees . . . .